BEAUTIFULLY TOXIC

CANDIED CRUSH #1

CHARITY PARKERSON

—Warning: This book is intended for readers over the age of 18.

Editor: BZ Hercules and Consultants
ISBN: 978-1-946099-71-6

Created with Vellum

INTRODUCTION

A FAMOUS DRUMMER. A HOMELESS TEEN. IT'S HARD TO TELL WHICH ONE IS THE SAVIOR.

When Jessie Thunder, a famous drummer, learns a homeless person has been sneaking into his home, Jessie decides to help him out. The eighteen-year-old "boy" is too old to go in the system, and Jessie can't stand the thought of anyone going hungry. He also hopes rescuing Theo will ease his soul. Otherwise, there's nothing redeeming left of him.

Even though Theo doesn't trust Jessie's help, he doesn't have anywhere else to go. At first, Jessie's attention feels like heaven. He's never had anyone care about him, especially someone as amazing as Jessie. Everything seems perfect. That is, until Theo realizes Jessie's beauty is only a mask. Inside, Jessie is poison and Theo has to get out before he finds himself in worse shape than when he lived on the street.

With Theo gone and no one to save him, Jessie has to make a choice. He can either rescue himself or drown in the toxic waste his life has become. Only one of those roads leads back to Theo.

Beautifully Toxic is the first book in bestselling author Charity Parkerson's series, Candied Crush, where the men are like candy—rich, irresistible, and bad for your health.

NOTE

This book contains heavy drug use.

ONE

It was rare for Jessie to be awake before noon. Yet, here he was awake and sober—like a double fuck you to his sanity. Jessie stared at his bedroom ceiling for half an hour before giving up on sleep. While the blackout curtains in his room kept him plunged in darkness, he could tell the sun shone brightly due to the sparkling Paris skyline. He didn't live anywhere near Paris. It was an illusion created by an artist friend of his. The tiny holes in the curtain made it look like lights were on in the Eiffel Tower. In reality, they showed a new day had come without Jessie's permission. Again. Damn, he was tired of waking up every day. Jessie was tired of showering, eating, and shitting. Life had a thousand tiny chores that drove him insane with boredom.

Jessie zoned out in the shower as notes started forming in his head. He needed to write them down before he forgot again. New songs came to him less and less these days. He was getting old. To most, thirty-four might not seem that old. To a man who had lived a hard rock lifestyle since his late teens, Jessie imagined his brain had been half pickled from the hardcore drugs and alcohol years ago. Jessie wasn't worried. He hadn't expected to live this long. Every day was a blessing, or a curse. However that saying went.

By the time Jessie dressed, he had already forgotten half the beats he had created in the shower. He trailed down the hallway and through the living room, trying to recapture his love for anything at all. Jessie had a feeling it was too late for all that.

As he cleared the kitchen doorway, Declan, the head of his security, looked up and froze with a huge spoonful of cereal halfway to his mouth. "Wow." Declan twisted his wrist to look at his watch, inadvertently dumping his next bite back into the bowl. Specks of milk splashed Declan's shirt. The gigantic dark-haired guy who had been at Jessie's side for years didn't seem to notice the mess he made. "It's nine a.m. When was the last time you saw this time of day?"

"Probably the same as the last time you saw your dick," Jessie quipped as he headed for the fridge.

A rumble of laughter followed Jessie. Declan was a big guy, but he wasn't fat, and they both knew it. Still, Jessie loved giving the guy hell about his size. Even though Jessie had never met Declan's parents, he was pretty sure one of them was a giant. As Jessie eyed the contents of the fridge, his long black hair fell in his face, reminding him he hadn't pulled it up yet. Since he wasn't hungry anyhow, Jessie gave up his hunt and pulled his hair into a ponytail before securing it with the hair tie from his wrist.

"Hey, by the way, I've been meaning to talk to you about your houseguest," Declan said, pulling Jessie's attention his way. "I know it's not unusual for you to bring home a stray for an extended stay, but this guy has been here two weeks. Do you plan to introduce him to security at some point?"

Jessie spent a moment trying to make Declan's words make sense. "I haven't brought anyone home in..." Jessie didn't know how to finish that. He couldn't recall the last time he had bothered with anyone at all.

For a moment, Declan stared at him in silence, as if giving Jessie time to remember he did in fact have a houseguest. "He's staying in the pool house," Declan tacked on unhelpfully.

A hint of irritation rose in Jessie. He might stay high a good eighty percent of the time, but he wasn't an idiot. "I'm telling you I don't have any guests."

A deep line appeared between Declan's eyebrows. He pushed to his feet. "Then who in the fuck is this guy?" He motioned Jessie over to the counter and flipped open his laptop. After a few clicks, Declan pulled up security footage of a guy entering the pool house.

Jessie moved closer to the screen as Declan played more clips of the same guy entering and leaving several times. "What the fuck? Who is that?"

"I don't know. He's been here for so long that we were certain you knew he was here."

"No." Jessie's gaze slid Declan's way. "Is he here right now?"

Declan nodded.

Jessie headed for the door. Nobody fucking broke into his place. This entire property was his blood and sweat. His soul. He had lost everything, including his sanity, for his place in the world.

For a big guy, Declan moved fast. He cut Jessie off before he made it to the back door. "Nope. You're not going out there. For all we know, this might be some crazed fan who would just love to kill you so they can keep your body for a fun time. It's time to be sane."

As much as Jessie wanted to storm the pool house and drag the unwanted guest out by his hair, he saw Declan's point. "You've got five minutes to fix this, or I will."

Declan rolled his eyes. Jessie got no respect. That was what he got for treating his employees like family. Declan dug out his cellphone and made a call. "Yeah. I need to report a break-in. No. They're still inside. I didn't call nine-one-one because it's not an emergency," Declan said, sounding irritated.

Jessie shook his head. "You called the police. Fuck that. I don't need the cops crawling around here." He headed for the door again.

Declan snatched him off his feet. It was ridiculous how easily he held Jessie in place with one hand while continuing his phone conversation like nothing happened.

"Come on, man. I'm gonna end up on *TMZ*."

"You're really gonna end up on TV if you go storming out there now. The police are sending someone. Just wait and watch. Everything will be fine. Let the cops do their job."

Jessie growled.

Declan huffed. "Do I need to lock you in your room like a little kid?"

"No, you don't need to lock me in my room like a little kid," Jessie said, sounding exactly like a little kid and incapable of stopping. This was his house. Some strange person was living in it. Jessie had every right to his anger. Someone needed to get pissed off. It may as well be him.

The police got there much faster than Jessie expected, but it was still enough time to make Jessie's rage grow. He watched from the window as they surrounded the pool house before storming the building. Declan stayed inside with Jessie. By the way Declan watched him, Jessie assumed he would get tackled to the floor if he tried to go outside.

Jessie stared at the open pool house door with his breath held. Shouts penetrated the walls, but Jessie couldn't make out their words. A few moments passed. Two policemen emerged with a handcuffed kid. Jessie leaned closer to the window. It had been hard to make out any details or features from their security footage. In the light of day, there was no mistaking the guy was no older than a teen. He looked eighteen at max, and that was pushing things.

"It's a kid." The shock was thick. It coated Jessie's mind, making it hard for him to think. The boy looked scared. His eyes were wild and his features sharp—like he had been starved. "What will they do with him?"

Declan shrugged. "I'm not sure. Take him to jail, I imagine. Would you like me to find out?"

"That's a kid," Jessie said, pointing toward the window. "I won't sleep again until I know what happened to him."

Declan released a loud sigh. "Don't move from this spot," he said, pointing at the floor. "You're not getting killed by some crazed fan on my watch."

"I won't move." Jessie meant it. He knew Declan wouldn't leave him alone otherwise, and Jessie needed to know the intruder's story.

With a sharp nod, Declan left him alone. Jessie stared so hard at the spot where Declan disappeared amongst the cops that his eyes watered. It felt like an eternity passed before Declan re-emerged and slipped back inside the house, closing the door behind him. Jessie held his breath until Declan's light green gaze focused on him.

"They're saying it's up to you. If you want to press charges, they'll take him in. If you don't, they can let him go."

Jessie's forehead furrowed. His irritation spiked. "What's he doing here?"

The way Declan kept his expression blank made Jessie wonder why Declan didn't want Jessie to know his thoughts. "He's homeless. It seems he was just looking for a warm place to sleep and stumbled onto the pool house when it was left unlocked. He doesn't even know who lives here."

"But he's a kid," Jesse automatically argued. Even he didn't know why he couldn't stop pointing out that detail. It just seemed wrong. "How does a kid end up homeless?"

"Actually, he's not a kid. He's eighteen. While he has no ID and all his worldly possessions are in a backpack in the pool house, I don't think he would have admitted to being an adult if he realized how much trouble he's in, so I have to think he's telling the truth. As to being homeless, he just aged out of a group home. The officer I talked to said he was what they refer to as a failed adoption. Some couple out there adopted him as a baby and then turned him back in at nine when they decided they didn't want to be parents after all. The guy says that's pretty common. Anyhow, by then, he was too old for anyone else to want him, so he lived in a group home until he turned eighteen. Then they turned him out. He had nowhere to go."

The sick feeling in Jessie's gut screamed he

needed to act. "What kind of people turn out a nine-year-old kid?"

Declan shrugged. "There are a lot of shitty people in this world, Jess. Not everyone takes in strays and loves them like kin the way you do." Declan glanced over his shoulder at the crowd gathered outside. "So what's the plan? Are you pressing charges?"

Jessie spent a moment chewing his bottom lip. He couldn't let the boy go to jail, but he also couldn't turn him out into the street. Jessie's gaze locked on Declan. "Hit the store and find him some clothes, shoes, toiletries, and whatnot. Pull off the tags. I doubt he'll accept them if he thinks they're new. I'll go deal with the cops."

Declan didn't budge from his spot, blocking the door. "What are you about to do?"

Jessie lifted one shoulder in a careless shrug. "I'm keeping him."

With a shake of his head, Declan pulled his phone from his back pocket. "Wait and let Johnny go with you just to be safe. All we have is this kid's word that he's not really some crazy person trying to get close to you."

Jessie smiled. He had known Declan all of his adult life, and he knew Declan believed he made the right decision. Otherwise, Jessie would already be locked in his room until this was over. The idea of doing right, even in the smallest way, warmed Jessie's heart. Most days, he didn't think he had much heart left. This was the right decision, though. Jessie felt it in his gut.

In hindsight, Theo recognized he had stayed in one spot too long. He should have known he would get busted crashing in such a sweet pad eventually. Damn, he hadn't expected the police to come busting in, waving guns and shouting threats. That was wild. Thankfully, they hadn't killed him, and now it looked like he would get three meals a day and a bed. He didn't imagine jail was all that different from a group home. Another day in the life of Theodor Harlow. Unwanted since birth. What a shitshow.

He kind of wished the cops would at least let him go to the bathroom, though. His bladder was about to burst. They had pumped him full of coffee and stuffed him with donuts while he waited to learn his fate. It was kind of funny in a way. He always thought people just went straight to jail. Instead, they were treating him like royalty. He was fairly close to Hollywood now. Maybe things were different here. Theo still couldn't believe he had survived the walk from San Diego. Six days of off and on walking with barely anything to drink and only what he found in the garbage to eat along the way had damn near killed him, but he had made it. His only friend, William, had left the group home six months ago. He had sworn he would give Theo a place to stay if Theo could make it to Los Angeles. Theo was here. William was nowhere to be found. Such was life. Abandoned again.

The police milling around him suddenly buzzed with excitement. Theo felt the change in the air. He was sitting sideways with his legs hanging out of the backseat of a cop car. They had taken off the handcuffs, but he wasn't free to go. Theo wanted to stand up and see what was going on, but he was scared to get shot. As hard as he tried to swallow down his fear and accept that he was about to go to jail, he didn't want to die today. Then the police parted, and Theo saw him. Long black hair. Whiskey eyes. The sexiest jawline Theo had ever seen in his life. Theo's eyes burned when he refused to blink against the sight of him. People kept stopping the new arrival and he kept signing things, smiling, and tossing glances Theo's way. Theo's skin heated. Every passing second, it got a little harder to breathe. By the time the crowd finally let the man reach Theo, Theo didn't even know his own name.

Those whiskey eyes focused on Theo. "Do you know who I am?"

Theo shook his head.

A way too sexy smile touched the man's lips. "I'm Jessie. It's my pool house you've been bunking in."

Horror washed over Theo. He rushed to try to make things right. "Oh, god. I'm so sorry. I swear I didn't mean any harm. I even slept on the floor so I wouldn't get the furniture dirty. It just gets a lot colder at night than I expected."

Jessie made a dismissive motion. "I'm not angry. In fact, I'm here to offer you a choice."

Theo's mouth went dry. He looked so nice. Theo couldn't look away. He was willing to bet Jessie was someone famous. Jessie was too beautiful not to be. "Okay."

"You can go with these guys or you can stay with me."

Confusion glued Theo's tongue to the roof of his mouth. Only because Theo hated to look like an idiot, he forced himself to speak. "I don't understand."

A kind smile tugged at Jessie's sexy lips. "I can't let you leave here with nowhere to go. So I can have these nice men leave you with me, and we can discuss you getting on your feet, or you can go with them. Either way, I can't let you go just to sleep in the street."

"Why?" God help Theo, he couldn't stop the question. No one ever did anything out of the kindness of their heart.

Jessie didn't even try to alleviate Theo's curiosity. "Which will it be? Me or jail?"

Holy shit. He was a wild beauty. Theo found himself leaning closer. "You."

The wicked smile that stretched Jessie's lips at Theo's response made Theo wonder if he had just agreed to sell his soul. He had never seen a man so tempting. Surely no good could come of this. At least he wasn't going to jail. That was the only comfort Theo could find. Now all he could do was wait to learn what the future would bring.

TWO

Jessie had not been expecting such a beautiful boy. He wanted to kick himself every time he had that thought. Theo was soft spoken. Tiny. Big and bright blue eyes. Shaggy brown hair. He was sweet, and Jessie was damn glad he hadn't let him go to jail. Jessie didn't think he would have survived. Theo hadn't stopped following Jessie around the house since the cops cleared out—like he worried about touching anything or that Jessie would think he had stolen something.

First, Jessie had Theo gather his things from the pool house and then he had found him an empty bedroom in the main house. Then Declan appeared with armfuls of clothes and toiletries. He dumped everything on Theo's new bed.

"This is Declan," Jessie said. "He's my bodyguard and driver. In truth, he handles everything. He's found some toiletries and some of my old clothes for you. There are towels in the bathroom, so you can get clean. That way, you don't have to feel guilty for sitting on the furniture."

Theo shifted from foot to foot. "Why do you need a bodyguard?"

The loud boom of laughter that Declan released nearly shook the walls. "Oh, I like him. He'll be good for your ego." Declan slapped his hands down on Jessie's shoulders and squeezed. "This here is *the* Jessie Thunder."

Theo looked even more uncomfortable. "I'm sorry. I don't recognize the name."

Declan snickered.

Jessie waved it off. "I was before your time."

"Liar," Declan muttered for Jessie's ears alone.

"I doubt that," Theo said, calling Jessie out as well. "You don't look much older than me."

It was Jessie's turn to aim a triumphant laugh in Declan's direction. "Ha. In your face. I told you I've still got it." When Jessie looked back Theo's way, Theo was smiling. Jessie's knees weakened. It happened so fast, he almost gave himself away. Theo had one of those sexy smiles with the deep lines beside his mouth. Jessie needed to give him space, but Theo wasn't having it.

"So do you plan to tell me who you are? I don't have any way to Google the name or anything like that."

"I was the drummer for Malice Abyss."

Theo nodded. "Is that a metal band? It sounds like a metal band."

Jessie couldn't stop smiling. For reasons he couldn't explain, he was beyond entertained by Theo. "Yeah. It's a metal band. Don't worry. There won't be a pop quiz. Declan and I will leave you alone so you can shower and relax. Whenever you're ready or feel comfortable, we'll be around." He headed for the door but paused as another thought hit. "By the way, there's security everywhere, so don't run away. We seriously only want to help. Okay?"

Theo nodded. His smile was gone. He looked sad—like he didn't trust Jessie's help. "Thank you. I won't run away."

Jessie smiled again, trying not to look threatening. He had already taken in one hurting boy when their mother died. This was familiar territory for him. Jessie just needed to think of this as the same as helping his little brother had been. He had to think of it that way. Otherwise, the too pretty

Theo would get him in a world of trouble. The last thing Jessie needed was another unshakable addiction. He already had more of those than he could count.

THEO DIDN'T DRAW A FULL BREATH UNTIL THE door closed behind Jessie. He turned in a slow circle, eyeing the room. Holy shit. He didn't know what to do. This was unreal. He shouldn't stay. These people were strangers. He couldn't take advantage of their kindness. His gaze slid toward the mound of clothes and whatnot on the bed. Maybe he could get clean, though. The past few weeks had been hell. Despite being unwanted, Theo hadn't gone hungry and been dirty like he was now. It was horrible. He had been turning the three sets of clothes he owned inside out for longer than anyone should have to such a thing. Jessie was offering him a respite. Theo didn't have the luxury of pride right now.

He didn't want to get anything dirty. He eased a hair closer. There was a plastic bag in the mix. Theo snagged it and looked inside. Shampoo, conditioner, body wash, toothpaste, an electric toothbrush, and deodorant, along with other odds and ends, overflowed the bag. The idea of being clean was too much to ignore. He headed for the bathroom. His feet froze to the floor at the first sight of the shower. It was a huge glass-encased work of art with multiple shower heads, jets, and seats. Theo moved closer, unsure of how to work the thing. With a chuckle, he started stripping. He trusted he could figure it out. Once nude, Theo found a couple of wash cloths and a towel. He dragged all the toiletries inside the shower and started turning knobs. After first scalding himself and then freezing himself, he finally managed to find a tolerable temperature from all the spouts. Theo scrubbed until his skin was blood red. He brushed his teeth in the shower because he wanted every inch of his body to be sparkling clean. Theo couldn't take another second of the filth. Each time he thought about getting out of the shower, Theo started scrubbing again. He washed his hair so many times, the shampoo was half gone by the time he convinced himself to turn off the water.

After talking himself from the shower, Theo made sure he was completely dry before returning to the bedroom. With a towel wrapped around his waist, Theo shifted through the clothes. He was ridiculously happy to see new and unopened socks and underwear. The pants were a little long, but the sizes were pretty dead on. There was an odd mixture of band t-shirts, polos, and tank tops. He picked a soft-looking t-shirt and jeans. Once dressed, he started folding clothes. Even though he was tired, Theo was too wired to sleep. So he put all the clothes in the dresser and the new shoes by the door. With everything put away, Theo found the hairbrush Declan had given him and started brushing. He still had his own hairbrush and whatnot in his backpack, but that was in the kitchen, and everything inside was dirty. Theo never wanted to be dirty again. He was already fighting the urge to get back in the shower.

With nothing else left for him to do to buy time, Theo squared his shoulders. He took a deep breath and opened the door. The house was huge. He took two wrong turns before things looked familiar. Theo was a little worried he wouldn't find his way back to his bedroom again. Finally, he heard voices and followed them. He spotted Declan first. The giant Viking-looking dude had his back to Theo as Theo slipped inside the room. The room fell silent. Declan turned and stepped aside, leaving Theo staring at Jessie. For a moment, Jessie stared back at him like he had forgotten what he was saying.

Theo waved like an idiot. "Hi. I found my way.

But I'm not sure I'll find my way back," Theo admitted with a wince.

A smile exploded across Jessie's face. "Declan or I will make sure you find your way back to your room when you're ready. It's not as confusing as it seems. We were just discussing stocking up on food. Any suggestions? I'm taking req—" The back door flew open and a tiny blond stormed in, blanking Theo's mind. He was the most beautiful man Theo had ever seen in his life.

"What the actual flock, Jessie? Why are all the news stations reporting that your house was crawling with police today?"

Jessie kissed the man's cheek and Theo had to look away. Of course. It made sense Jessie would be dating someone so gorgeous. He had perfect pink highlights running through his light hair. Everything about him was flawless.

"Meet our new houseguest." At Jessie's words, Theo forced his chin up, refusing to be weak. Jessie motioned Theo's way. "This is Theo. Theo, meet my baby brother, Ezra."

Relief washed over Theo. He didn't want to look too closely at why. Theo automatically swiped his hands on his thighs in a show of nerves. "Nice to meet you, Ezra. It's my fault the police were here. I'm sorry if I scared you."

Ezra glanced Jessie's way. "Oh, he's adorable." Without waiting for a response from Jessie, Ezra bounded across the kitchen. "It's so nice to meet you too. Why would the police be here for you? I could think of a million better reasons."

Heat rushed to Theo's face. "Um. I guess I sort of broke in."

That seemed to draw Ezra up short. He blinked several times before finding his voice. "Are you a huge fan of Malice Abyss?"

"He's never heard of Jessie," Declan chimed in with a chuckle.

Ezra tossed a laughing look Declan's way. "Really? How delicious."

"I was just looking for a place to sleep," Theo admitted. He didn't want to make Ezra dig.

Ezra's smile fell as his gorgeous hazel eyes latched on to Theo again. "Oh, sweetie. Are you homeless?"

The heat in Theo's cheeks doubled. The humiliation was real. He felt so overly exposed. Before today, Theo hadn't thought he had any pride left to bruise. These amazing people were setting fire to what little he had left to burn.

Jessie came to his rescue. "Theo isn't homeless. He belongs to us now."

Ezra's gaze swung between them. Theo fought the urge to run. He felt completely useless and small. To his surprise, Ezra leapt forward and hugged him. "Yay. I'm so happy you're joining our rag-tag family." The hug happened so fast, Theo didn't have time to hug him back. It was a fact Theo was grateful for when he caught sight of Declan's expression. He looked possessive and like he watched Theo's hands to make sure they stayed respectful. Theo made a mental note of that, since Declan could likely kill him in one blow.

Ezra seemed blind to the tension. He kept smiling like he had just met his new best friend. "So why is everyone standing around the kitchen? Are we discussing dinner options? If so, I vote pizza. I know it's a little early to be eating dinner already, but I'm starving. I just finished a photoshoot and I've been depriving myself for weeks. Now it's time to get fat."

"Photoshoot?" Theo asked.

Declan spoke over him. "You are not supposed to be starving yourself. What the hell, Ezra? When you started this modeling gig, you promised Jessie and me that you wouldn't starve yourself. Sit down. I'll fix you a sandwich."

Ezra huffed. "I said I've been depriving myself. That's not the same as giving up food entirely. Just let me steal some of Johnny's peanuts from his hidden stash, and we can order some pizza. I don't want a sandwich." Ezra opened a cabinet above his head next to the refrigerator.

Declan ripped open the refrigerator door, looking ready to snap. "Fine, but I'm getting you a soda. Full sugar. No diet shit. So just deal." Declan quickly rose from the fridge and turned. A little too quick. Ezra still had the cabinet door open. When Declan turned to hand Ezra the soda, he got hit in the face with the cabinet door.

"Holy ship. Are you okay? I'm so sorry." Despite Declan's repeated assurances he was fine, Ezra pulled Declan's face down to his so he could inspect his eye. He kept Declan's face cupped between his hands. "Oh, sweetie. You already have a little bruise forming. I'm a terrible person." He pressed his lips to the spot where Declan had been hit.

Declan's arm shot out and his knuckles collided with the edge of the counter as he fought for purchase. Theo had never seen anyone punched so hard by desire, while no one else seemed to notice but Theo. Theo cast a glance Jessie's way, hoping for a moment of commiseration. Jessie was leaned against the counter on the opposite side of the kitchen, playing on his phone. A wave of loneliness washed over Theo. His entire life had been exactly like this. He saw too much, but no one saw him. Theo was always alone, no matter how many people surrounded him. His burden felt even heavier today.

JESSIE KEPT HIS GAZE LOCKED ON HIS PHONE because it was the safe choice. Theo was drop dead gorgeous. Nothing good could come of inviting this beautiful boy to live with him. The first sight of a clean Theo nearly broke Jessie's brain. As soon as he finished mentally berating himself for his reaction, and decided he would ignore Theo's sexiness, Ezra had burst in. Ezra had always been the most stunning person in every room. Witnessing Theo's reaction to seeing Ezra for the first time was hell. White-hot jealousy had risen in Jessie's chest. He fought the urge to scream Theo was his. Jessie had found him. Finders keepers.

Jessie lifted his gaze from his phone. Big blue eyes were focused on him. Theo looked sad. Jessie couldn't see anyone else. He immediately set his phone aside. "What do you say, gorgeous? Do you like pizza?"

Theo looked around, as if trying to decide who Jessie was talking to, while Jessie mentally berated himself again. Fucking coke had him saying his every thought. He needed to get his shit together.

Jessie decided the best thing to do was roll with it —like he called everyone gorgeous all the time. "Yo, Theo. I'm talking to you. Do you like pizza?"

Theo met his stare again. His cheeks pinked. "Yes."

Ezra jumped up and down and grabbed Theo's hand. He dragged Theo toward the table. "Yay. I'm so glad you're here. Jessie only lets me have my way like ninety percent of the time. It's obvious you're the co-conspirator I've been needing to get that other ten percent."

Jessie rolled his eyes and grabbed his phone before claiming the chair on the other side of Theo. While turned sideways in his seat, Jessie dragged Theo's chair closer to his. Theo looked like he scrambled not to fall while Jessie manhandled him, but fuck it. Jessie wasn't letting his little brother steal his new toy. He opened the search engine on his phone and looked up pizza joints. "Help me choose."

Jessie hoped his demand made his manhandling look less like he was beating his chest. "What's your favorite pizza spot?"

For a moment, Theo held Jessie's stare, making his heart beat a little faster. Theo barely spared the phone a glance before shrugging. "I don't know any of the places here."

Confusion had Jessie's forehead furrowing. "How is that possible? Surely you've had pizza before."

A smile lit Theo's features that stole Jessie's breath. "Of course I have, but I'm from San Diego."

"How did you get here?" The question popped from Jessie without his permission. Even to his ears, he sounded kind of dickish. Thankfully, Theo didn't stop smiling.

"I walked."

"From San Diego?" Jessie might have half yelled. He had no volume control while high.

Theo nodded. "It's not like I had anything else to do."

"We're going to order for the rest of the security team too. Do you have any particular type—like all meats or whatever that you like best?" Ezra asked Theo, cutting in.

Theo glanced his way. "All the meats works for me."

Ezra nodded but didn't look up from his phone.

Theo's laughing gaze swung back Jessie's way. "It looks like Ezra has things under control."

"He usually does." Jessie felt like he was falling into the blue of Theo's eyes. He shook his head, trying to shake off the feeling before he did something stupid. "Help me make a grocery list instead," Jessie said, opening his notebook app and forcing his attention elsewhere. "I want you to be happy here."

"I don't know why you're doing this, but thank you."

Jessie found himself focused on Theo's sexy eyes again at his claim. A smile tugged at his lips. He wouldn't leave Theo guessing at his intentions. "Everyone here is an orphan of some kind. Ezra and I were raised by a single mother. We have different fathers, but neither of us knows who they are. Mom was kind of a wild woman," he added with a chuckle. "She died when Ezra was fifteen and so I raised him. Declan has been with me since I first started out on the road. He was seventeen and a drop-out with abusive parents. Johnny, you'll meet him eventually, I hired him off the streets when he jumped in front of a guy who tried to throw a drink at me. There are a dozen people here with similar stories." Jessie shrugged. "I don't know why I'm like this, but I am. Sometimes, people don't have anyone else. I have plenty of space. Maybe I'm an addict with a temper and almost zero fucks. I'm also definitely no saint, running a place for wayward people, but I'll help you if I can."

Theo visibly swallowed and looked away. "You have no idea how much I appreciate it. I was out of options and low on hope when I found your pool house."

"We've got you," Ezra said, rubbing Theo's arm and stealing his attention again. "Jessie went hungry many times as a kid. Now that he has more money than God, he won't let anyone in his care starve."

"You'll be happy here." Even Jessie heard the hard edge to his voice, as if it was more of a threat than a promise.

Still, with his gaze locked on his lap, Theo smiled. Something in Jessie's chest shifted. He didn't understand why he felt so immediately drawn to and protective of Theo, but he did. If Theo would let him, Jessie would make sure he had an amazing life.

THEO'S NEW BED WAS SO COMFORTABLE THAT HE couldn't sleep. Plus, thoughts of Jessie ran through his head. All night, Jessie had sat too close. Smelled too good. Since Theo still really didn't know who Jessie was to the world, he didn't think he was star struck. He supposed his all-over-the-place emotions could be hero worship. No one had ever rescued him. At least, not that he remembered. Theo fully recalled being abandoned, though. He remembered his adoptive parents' faces. Their impatience. Their neglect. Theo forced his thoughts back Jessie's way. At some point in the night, between the pizza and breaking out the video games, Jessie had slipped away. Theo hadn't even gotten to tell him goodnight. He was a little sad about that and didn't know why.

Theo's bedroom door burst open, sending Theo's heart racing into his throat. Jessie stepped inside and flipped on the lights. He had a couple of boxes against his chest and looked lit brighter than a Christmas tree. "Jesus Christ, darling. What kind of eighteen-year-old goes to bed at..." He moved his watch really close to his face. "...two a.m.? That can't be right. Anyhow," Jessie said, focusing on Theo once more. "You said you can't Google me, and I really don't want you to. Also, don't search Ezra's name either, or you'll see some really very nude pics that he doesn't know I know about. Other than that, I want you to have a normal life, which includes internet. Plus, I want to be able to talk to you whenever I want to talk to you. So, tada." Jessie held the boxes out to Theo as Theo sat up in the bed.

"What's this?"

Jessie dumped the boxes in Theo's lap and climbed into bed with him. "It's a phone and laptop. Welcome to modern times." Jessie flopped down on his stomach beside Theo and closed his eyes.

Theo looked at the haul. Since he had never had a way to get to a job, he had never worked. Which meant he had never had money for electronics. Well, not anything nice. When he had left the group home, he had bought a prepaid phone so he could call William when he got to L.A. William hadn't answered and Theo had run out of minutes leaving voicemails. Even though he hadn't owned anything nice, that didn't mean he didn't know what the best brands were. The laptop and phone were the most expensive on the market.

"I can't accept these."

"Shut up, gorgeous," Jessie mumbled, sounding half asleep. "My money. My choices."

Theo didn't know an argument for that one, so he broke the seal on the phone. The complicated device made him feel like an idiot. "This thing wants me to set up a code. What should I use?"

"An important date, I suppose."

Theo tried to think, but nothing came to mind. "I'll just use today's date." After all, it had definitely been a day he wouldn't forget. "It wants to use my face too. Sheesh, you would think one code would be enough." Theo did all the chin up, down, and face side to side as prompted. It seemed to take forever. "It wants me to connect to the internet."

Jessie's head shot up. His eyes were barely open. "It's the one named Windowless White Van."

Theo chuckled as he clicked on it. "Got it."

Jessie nodded. "The password is I'm not fucking playing with you. All one word. All caps."

Once he was online, Theo suddenly felt like the world was at his fingertips. Jessie shot up—like someone stabbed him. "Hold on. Let me text you so you'll have my number." He dug out his phone and started typing.

As the phone in Theo's hand buzzed, Jessie flopped back down and closed his eyes. Theo opened his text.

Jessie: *Now I'm always at your fingertips.*

Theo smiled like an idiot. A soft snore came from Jessie's side of the bed. Without thought, Theo reached over and smoothed Jessie's hair away from his face. He tucked the strands behind Jessie's ear. Theo swore his heart sighed. It wasn't like he was an idiot. Jessie was out of his league and obviously an addict. But Theo wasn't insane. No one in their right mind would miss their chance to touch him.

"There he is," Declan said, appearing in Theo's doorway. Theo immediately pulled his hand back—like he had been burned. Declan crossed the room. "I'll get him out of here."

"He's fine."

Declan snorted. "Trust me. You don't want him waking up in here. The comedown from this big of a high is ugly. Let him keep his pride, babe."

Guilt washed over Theo. Jessie had been so kind. Theo shouldn't want more. He flashed Declan a smile. "Of course. I'm sure he'd happier in his own bed."

Theo watched with his heart in his throat as Declan slung Jessie over his shoulder and carried him from the room. He knew there was no way he would sleep now from worrying about Jessie. He hated that Jessie was obviously messed up. It felt wrong for someone so gorgeous to have anything but a beautiful life. Everyone had some type of cross to bear. Even the rich and otherwise perfect, it seemed.

THREE

As hard as Theo tried, he didn't make it past eight a.m. before venturing from his room. His stomach wouldn't stop growling. It was like having a big dinner reminded him what it was like to eat properly. Theo needed to forage while everyone else was—hopefully—still sleeping. He had an easier time finding his way to the kitchen this time. His stomach led the way. Thankfully, the house was quiet and seemingly empty. He didn't have to feel guilty for blatantly searching the cabinets.

They had left a huge mess last night. Pizza boxes and soda bottles had littered the kitchen while they had crowded the theater room and played VR games for the rest of the night until Jessie disappeared. This morning, the place sparkled and smelled clean—like they had never been there. The sunlight pouring in through the windows and French doors made the huge kitchen feel homelike. It was odd to Theo that this house felt more like home in one night than the group home had in nine years. He knew he couldn't stay here forever, but damned if it didn't feel like a forever home.

One side of Jessie's massive kitchen had tons of cabinets. As Theo blatantly searched them, he realized the grocery list he had made with Jessie last night had magically become reality. His favorite ultra-sugary cereal stared out at him. A huge smile stretched his lips as he grabbed the box. He felt like a little kid as he went on the hunt for a bowl and spoon. When he opened the fridge, he found even more of the items he had suggested. Jessie was like some kind of fairy godfather.

Theo was settled on a barstool at the island and on his second humongous bowl of cereal when Declan made an appearance. He smiled sleepily at Theo as he headed for the fridge. Theo smiled back as he chewed.

Declan glanced at Theo's bowl as he poured himself some orange juice. "Would you like some bacon with that?"

Theo shook his head. He didn't want to admit he

had already eaten half a box of cereal. "I'm good. Thank you, though."

With a nod, Declan grabbed a bowl and joined Theo at the bar. Theo fought not to look Declan's way when Declan grabbed the box of cereal and started pouring. He didn't want to see the guy's judgment over how much he had already eaten. They chewed in companionable silence for several minutes.

"I haven't had this brand of cereal in years," Declan said between bites. "I forgot how good it is."

Before Theo could respond, the back door opened, and Ezra stepped inside. "Oh, good. You're up."

Theo had no idea which of them he meant, so he didn't respond. A movement from the corner of Theo's eye caught his attention. He glanced over to find a small blond guy making his way down the hall. He was pretty. That didn't explain who he was or why he was there. The guy's hazel eyes swept from side to side, taking in the scene before landing on Ezra, which made perfect sense to Theo. He was the prettiest.

"Who are you?"

"Jessie's brother," Ezra said so fast, it cleared

everything up to Theo's mind. This guy had come from Jessie's bedroom.

The guy's gaze moved Theo's way. His eyebrows rose.

Theo tried not to flinch under his judgmental stare. "Jessie's houseguest." Theo hoped that would be enough to pacify the jealousy in the man's stare.

Declan jumped to his feet before he found himself the center of the same inquest. "I'll see you out."

Theo watched Declan walk outside with the stranger. It was ridiculous for Theo to be hurt, but he kind of was. Knowing he was being dumb didn't do a thing for Theo's sanity. For a few hours last night, Jessie had sat so close, and Theo had dreamed. Damn. He was really stupid.

Ezra took control, saving Theo from the lump growing in his throat. "I've come to steal you for the day. I need a partner in crime. We're talking mani-pedis, hair done, and full facials. The works."

That was enough to distract Theo. "I don't have any money."

Ezra snorted. "I didn't say anything about you needing money. My treat."

Guilt ate Theo alive, stinging his pride. "I can't accept all that."

"Don't worry about it. It's not my money. It's Jessie's. Models don't make any money." He tilted his head from side to side, as if rethinking his claim, before adding, "Except for those photos Jessie doesn't know about." A wicked smile stretched Ezra's lips. "I made a lot of money for those." He seemed to snap back to reality. "Anyhow, I've got you. Get your shoes and let's go."

Since Ezra seemed excited, Theo slipped from the stool and headed down the hall. Back at his room, he found some socks and the shoes Declan had given him. They were a half size too big, but Theo was literally the definition of beggars couldn't be choosers. With his shoes laced up, Theo's gaze slid toward his new phone. It wasn't like anyone would call him, but he still found himself slipping it in his pocket before rushing back out to meet Ezra.

Declan was back at the island. He ate his cereal while staring intently at the window above the sink. Ezra stood on the opposite side of the kitchen, as if trying to stay as far away from Declan as possible. Unlike yesterday, where they had been in each other's pockets, this morning, the tension was palpable. It was like they were angry and trying to ignore each other. They were a puzzle.

Ezra smiled when he caught sight of Theo. "Yay. We're going to have so much fun."

Theo wasn't sure facials were his idea of fun, but he would give it a shot for Ezra's sake. "I'm looking forward to it."

They headed for the door with Ezra in the lead, taking charge.

Declan cleared his throat. It was an uncomfortable sound. "Be careful. You know how traffic is here."

Ezra completely ignored him. Theo kept his head down, hoping to avoid the crossfire. Ezra led him to a white Audi S7 and motioned for Theo to get in. "Your carriage, good sir."

Theo realized he was smiling. He genuinely liked Ezra. Of course, he doubted there was a soul alive who didn't like Ezra. The moment Theo was strapped in, Ezra became a hurricane. He talked a mile a minute and drove like a grandma. Everywhere they went, they were greeted with smiles and treated like royalty. Two hours in, Theo's phone chirped, nearly making him jump out of his skin. He dug out the device and checked his messages.

Jessie: *Where did you disappear to?*

Theo fought a wave of happiness. Blond overnight guest forgotten. He glanced Ezra's way.

"It's Jessie. He wants to know where I've gone." Theo didn't know why he explained his text. It just seemed rude to be on his phone during their outing without telling him why. He started typing, letting Jessie know where he had gone. He was slow and the phone kept autocorrecting his words, but he finally managed. Before he could get his phone put away, another text rolled in.

Jessie: *Tell Ezra to make sure he keeps both his hands on the wheel.*

"Jessie says for you to make sure you keep both your hands on the wheel."

The foils in Ezra's hair caught the light as he looked Theo's way. His eyes danced with laughter. "Tell him he has nothing to worry about. I'm not blind. I read all the signs and saw the sparks."

Even though he was confused as hell, Theo typed Ezra's message word for word. He didn't have long to wait for a response.

Jessie: *Good. See you soon. BTW, I'm sorry I passed out in your bed last night.*

Theo bit his lip. Damn. He was scared of the happiness. Theo wasn't used to feeling like this.

Theo: *It's okay. I'm just glad you're up and moving this morning.*

"What did he say?"

Theo answered without thought. "That he's sorry for passing out in my bed last night." Horror raced through Theo the moment the words left him. He wanted to snatch them back, but it was too late. Still, he tried. "I did not mean that how it sounded. He popped in to give me this phone and then passed out."

The laughter etched in Ezra's every feature couldn't be missed. "You don't have to explain. I know my brother. No matter how fucked up he gets, he's not the type to take advantage of you. Plus, he's on so much stuff, he probably hasn't been able to get it up in years."

Theo blinked. Part of him wanted to remind Ezra of the blond who had been a half a second away from a jealous rage this morning. The rest of Theo couldn't believe Ezra would talk about anyone getting it up. In the end, he decided to tackle the rest of Ezra's claim. "Do you worry about him?"

Ezra stared at his own reflection as he answered. "Constantly, but life isn't easy for anyone. He's grown and he's still a functioning addict. No one is having to Narcan ten times a day and I call that a win."

Theo stared at his reflection in the mirror while he waited for his stylist. He couldn't stop comparing his life from two days ago to now. These people were so different from anyone he had ever met, yet they were the same. A higher class of unhappy. They had money and endless options, but they still had to survive everyday life, which—apparently—sucked ass for everyone equally. The last couple of days had been enlightening. Still, Theo wouldn't trade them for the world. But it was a little ridiculous how badly he wanted to go home to Jessie. He was in so much trouble.

FOUR

After two hours of hugging the toilet, Jessie thought he might live. He didn't feel confident enough to go hunting for Theo until he survived the world's longest shower. Jessie still couldn't believe he had passed out in the boy's bed on his first night. Theo had to think he had jumped out of the frying pan and into the fire by trusting Jessie. The last thing Jessie wanted was for Theo to be scared of him. Unfortunately, it hadn't taken him much searching to realize Theo was gone. Jessie's first thought was Theo had disappeared back into the streets, leaving Jessie with no way to find him. Thankfully, Theo had taken his cellphone and set Jessie's mind at ease immediately. Of course, that did nothing for his boredom. So Jessie ended up doing what he always did. He paced and popped pills.

By the time Theo came through the back door, Jessie almost rushed him and yanked him off his feet. He was so damn relieved to have company. Then he got a good look at him. Lust hit him like a sledgehammer. He checked his t-shirt to make sure it hid his instant erection. Jessie was so goddamn surprised, he imagined he looked like an idiot stopping midway through his greeting. He hadn't experienced an iota of desire in over a year. Jessie didn't even bother trying any longer. Yet here Theo was, looking innocent and shy, and Jessie's body acted like he was watching hardcore porn. Those blue eyes, though, and they had done something to his hair... fuck.

Jessie tried killing his lust by talking about his brother. "Where'd you lose Ezra?"

Theo's entire face lit—like seeing Jessie brightened his whole life, and Jessie knew in that moment he was completely fucked. "He said to tell you he'll call you later."

"That's cool. So it's just us." Fuck his entire life, even he heard the threat in his voice. He tried playing it off. "Come on. I want to show you something."

"Okay." Theo pulled at his clothes subconsciously.

Jessie motioned Theo down a different hallway toward the opposite end of the house from the bedroom he had assigned Theo. "It's this way. You look nice, by the way," he added as he led Theo away. He didn't look to see how his compliment landed. Jessie was fully aware that he was nearly twenty years older than Theo and couldn't act on the way the guy heated his skin. Truthfully, Jessie was more confused than anything. It wasn't like Theo was a model or a porn star. He was just some barely classified as an adult guy who had fallen in Jessie's lap. Jessie didn't know why Theo made him want to give him everything and see him smile. For half a second yesterday, helping Theo had been about being a good human. Now Jessie just couldn't look away from him, and he needed to know why.

As Jessie cleared the doorway of his studio, the lights automatically flared to life. Jessie turned and walked backward into the room. "Welcome to my studio."

Theo tried looking in every direction at once. "Wow. This is amazing. You must be a phenomenal talent."

Jessie picked up a pair of drumsticks and

motioned toward the production booth. "That's where the real magic happens. I'm just some guy with two sticks."

Theo rolled his eyes and headed for the booth. Jessie couldn't stop smiling while he watched Theo inspecting everything. Theo ran his hand across the panel of knobs and buttons, as if scared he would mess something up. "Oh my god. This place is unreal. I can't even fathom how much a person would have to know to do this. You must be a musical genius. An exhausted one. I'm speechless."

People rarely thought about how much work went into his job. That point being the first thing Theo mentioned was moving. Jessie tried not to show it. "Do you like music?"

Theo shrugged. "As much as the next person, I guess."

A smile snapped to Jessie's lips. "But you're not passionate about it," he surmised.

Theo's expression turned guilty—like he thought he was letting Jessie down for some reason. "Here you are, this famous drummer, and I don't usually even know the names of the songs I like, much less the band's name. Sorry." Theo winced at the confession.

He was adorable. "Don't apologize. Not

everyone loves the same things. That's what makes the world beautiful and unique. What are you passionate about?"

Theo blushed and tried hiding it. Jessie couldn't look away. "I don't have any talents. I'm just me. I'm pretty useless, actually."

He didn't like Theo talking bad about himself. Jessie moved closer. Theo's scent had him taking measured breaths. He smelled delicious. Jessie needed to thank Ezra for pampering Theo today. He tried staying on topic. "Don't say that, and I wasn't referring to talent. I mean, what do you love? Movies? Skateboarding? Computers? Books? All the above? None of the above? What would you buy every single one of, if you could afford it?"

Theo seemed to think it over, as if no one had asked him about himself before. Suddenly, his expression turned whimsical. A small smile touched his lips as his gaze slid Jessie's way. Jessie found himself holding his breath, needing to hear Theo's thoughts. "I used to have a huge comic book collection." He spread his arms wide, as if trying to impress upon Jessie exactly how massive this collection was. "I don't know if they were actually worth anything. I doubt they were, but I treated them like they were priceless." Theo's smile turned sad. His gaze turned inward. "When Ted and Suzie left me at the hospital, they kept everything. They returned me with only the clothes on my back." Theo shook his head. "I haven't thought about that in years."

Jessie's throat swelled. His mind latched on to one detail and churned furiously with it. *They returned me with only the clothes on my back.* Like an unwanted item from the store or a puppy that hadn't worked out. Jessie wanted to find these people and destroy them. Theo was a person and he had been reduced to a returnable item. The amount of rage Jessie felt at the tolerant way Theo talked about the inhumane manner he had been treated doubled Jessie's rage. Theo accepted his abuse like it was Tuesday. It took every ounce of Jessie's willpower not to explode like a psychopath. He kept twirling his drumsticks, trying to focus on anything else. An idea hit.

"We should get Declan to take us to a comic book store."

Theo flashed him a sweet smile. "That's okay. I don't have any money. I'd rather hear you play instead."

His mind whirled. He would have to find a way to give Theo some money without hurting his pride.

For now, he let it drop. "If that's what you'd like." Jessie headed for his favorite drum set. He pointed one stick toward the panel on the left. "Hit that green button at the top. Then spin that black dial at the bottom." While Jessie settled behind the drums, Theo moved to sit at the panel and did as told. A guitar solo filled the air. Jessie tapped his foot. The music flowed through him. He matched the beat without thought. It was as automatic as breathing for Jessie. Familiar vocals joined in and Jessie was gone. He disappeared inside the music—his real home. Jessie was back on stage. He swore he could feel the roar of the crowd. His motions never wavered. It was an art. The song changed. The beat slowed, transitioning into one of the band's most popular love songs. It was heartbreak and loss. Tragedy. Jessie felt each chord in his soul. Then his gaze met Theo's and he was back in reality. Jessie played for Theo and Theo alone. They were connected. Theo looked enthralled—like Jessie had swept him into the same escape Jessie had enjoyed for a moment. Realization struck like lightning. Jessie wanted to sweep Theo away. He wanted to show Theo the world. He needed Theo to smile and mean it. Maybe his intentions had been pure when he had taken Theo in, but they weren't anymore. There was nothing pure about the way he felt with Theo watching him now. That was exactly why he needed to stop.

"When is your birthday?"

Theo rapidly blinked at Jessie's jump from playing the drums to being done in an instant. "It was a month ago. You're insanely talented. I'm not surprised you got famous."

Jessie ignored the compliment. "If your birthday was a month ago, I missed getting you a gift."

A humorless smile touched Theo's lips. "You didn't know me a month ago."

"So?"

"So what?" Theo asked when Jessie didn't say more.

"What do you want for your birthday?" Jessie killed the music, giving Theo time to think.

"I don't want anything."

Jessie rolled his eyes. He took Theo's hands and pulled him to his feet. "Everyone wants something. What do you want?"

An uncomfortable-sounding laugh burst from Theo. "Nothing. I'm good. Plus, you gave me a phone and laptop last night. You've already done too much for me."

"Those weren't presents. They were necessities." Jessie's head spun. He rubbed his eyes. "Fuck." He dug a pill from his pocket and swallowed it without water. "Let's get Declan. We're going to get you a gift."

Theo tried arguing, but Jessie walked away. He wasn't hearing it. Theo was good. He deserved nice things. Jessie wouldn't return him like those scumbags who adopted him. Theo had a new family here. Jessie could buy him things. "Woot. Woot," Jessie yelled as loud as he could, making sure Declan knew they were headed out and needed to get his shit together. Jessie wasn't known for his patience.

"I'm coming," Declan growled, stumbling down the hall. Jessie didn't feel guilty. He paid a lot of money for Declan to be at his beck and call twenty-four hours a day. "Where we headed?" Declan asked as he stamped into a pair of worn work boots.

"We missed Theo's birthday. He has to pick out a gift."

"I don't really want anything," Theo muttered behind him, sounding despondent.

"Chin up, baby. You're getting a present. I'd drive you myself, but I haven't been sober since before you were born."

Jessie wasn't satisfied until everyone had their shoes on and were loaded into the black Mercedes-AMG G63 they took everywhere.

"Where are we headed?" Declan asked again as he pulled from the garage.

Theo looked determined to stay quiet.

"Fine. You'll get what you're getting, then. Pick up Ezra. We're going to dinner. I need time to think of the perfect present."

"Ezra's it is."

Jessie nodded. He would give Theo the perfect birthday whether the boy liked it or not. One of them should be happy. In the ten-minute drive to Ezra's, Jessie stared at Theo's profile. He was pretty. Pretty boys deserved pretty things.

"You look like music."

Theo glanced his way. Laughter swam in his eyes. "What?"

"Music," Jessie repeated. "Like you could make music. You'll see."

Theo shook his head. It was obvious Jessie confused him.

Jessie knew, though. "Stop by Touch of Gold. I know what to get."

Declan changed lanes and turned at the light. "I think they close in like five minutes."

Jessie wasn't worried. "Five minutes is all I need. I know exactly what I want." Theo looked at him with raised eyebrows. Jessie wagged his finger at him.

"Nope. You have to wait." Jessie dug his pills from his pocket. "Did I take this?" He didn't wait for an answer. "Not that it matters." He popped another pill as Declan screeched to a halt in front of Touch of Gold. Jessie tossed Theo a quick glance. "Wait here. I'll be right back." Jessie leapt from the SUV and headed inside with Declan following closely behind. He focused on the first salesman he saw. "I need a necklace."

The guy shook his head, as if shaking off his shock at the sight of Jessie. Jessie was used to that reaction. Unlike Theo's first reaction to meeting him. He genuinely hadn't known who Jessie was when they met. Jessie fought a smile and forced himself to focus on the salesman's words. "Of course, Mr. Thunder. What did you have in mind?"

Jessie made a dismissive motion. At least, he thought he did. Declan jumped back a foot as if he had almost gotten hit. Jessie ignored him. "It's just Jessie. Gold, high quality, durable, and with a musical note charm."

"Nice." At Declan's claim, Jessie flashed him a smile.

"I have the perfect thing," the salesman said, moving to unlock a nearby display case. He pulled out a gold chain with a music note hanging from it.

Jessie leaned close and eyed the necklace. It was perfect. The chain was long enough it wouldn't choke Theo, and thick enough it wouldn't break easily. Yet, it was thin enough to look amazing against Theo's skin. A smile stretched Jessie's lips. "Yep. That's it." He dug for his wallet and pulled out a black card. Jessie passed it the guy's way.

"Do you need a box?"

Jessie shook his head. "Just ring me up and I'll get out of your hair."

With the receipt signed, Jessie headed back out to where he had left Theo. Rather than climbing inside, he circled the SUV and opened Theo's door. Theo blinked at him like he had lost his mind. Then his gaze landed on the necklace Jessie held. His lips parted in surprise.

Jessie motioned for Theo to lean forward. "Come here. I'll put it on."

Theo didn't budge. "You can't give that to me."

Irritation had Jessie pinning Theo in place with his stare. "I can and I am. Happy goddamn birthday. Now lean forward and let me put this on you."

Theo dutifully leaned forward. While Jessie worked the clasp, Theo's closeness and warmth sank in. Jessie's lips touched the shell of Theo's ear with no permission from Jessie's brain. "Happy birthday, baby. I hope you like it."

Theo leaned away and looked down as if checking out the necklace. He wasn't quick enough, though. Jessie caught sight of the tears in Theo's eyes before he could hide them. "It's beautiful. Thank you."

Jessie kissed the top of Theo's head. "Let's get dinner."

Theo nodded, but he didn't look up from the necklace. Jessie knew then he had made the right choice. Someone moved by such a small gift deserved that and so much more. Jessie would give him a good life. He would see.

THEO COULDN'T TAKE HIS EYES OFF THE necklace Jessie gave him. Declan couldn't take his eyes off Ezra and Jessie was too high to see a thing. By the time they were headed home, Theo asked Declan to drop them off first and then take Ezra home. Otherwise, Theo was scared Jessie would pass out in public and end up on the news. Since Jessie was too out of it to answer, and Declan seemed more than happy to have Ezra to himself, he obliged.

Once they were home, they didn't make it past the living room. Jessie kicked off his shoes and started peeling off clothes. "Is it hot? I'm hot."

Theo tried keeping him calm. "Maybe you just need some water. I'll get you some water."

Jessie waved off Theo's suggestion. Instead, he stumbled through the darkened room toward the couch. "I don't need water. I just need to sit down."

On autopilot, Theo followed Jessie to the couch, determined to catch him if he fell. He kept a light tone, trying to hide his worry. "Thank you again for everything tonight. The necklace is beautiful, and I had a great time."

Jessie flashed him a smile as he dropped onto the couch. He pulled Theo down beside him and draped his arm over Theo's shoulders. "You're good people and good people deserve nice things."

Theo shook his head. Jessie was always nice. Since a fucked-up mouth spoke a sober mind, Theo had to believe Jessie was truly kind all the way to his soul. Theo found himself snuggling against Jessie's side, even though he knew he shouldn't. Jessie was warm and Theo liked being touched. "You smell good." Theo sniffed Jessie's bare chest like a full-on perv. He didn't care anymore. Pride was out the window. Plus, he didn't imagine Jessie would remember any of this by morning anyway. He was more fucked up than Theo had ever seen anyone.

A sexy-sounding chuckle rumbled from Jessie. "I've never met anyone like you. You say whatever you're thinking with no filter. It's refreshing."

"I'm sorry." Even Theo didn't know why he was apologizing. No filter sounded a lot like he shouldn't have said what he said, which was true, but still.

Jessie touched Theo's chin and forced Theo to meet his gaze. Despite being out of his head, Jessie's whiskey eyes looked sober in that moment. "Never apologize for being yourself." Jessie's gaze dropped to Theo's mouth. He traced Theo's bottom lip with his thumb. "I like you just as you are." A sardonic smile touched Jessie's lips. "I'm thirty-four. That's old enough to be your dad," he muttered, as if talking to himself. He dropped his hand and looked away.

An unexpected bark of laughter burst from Theo. "Not really. Unless you started really young."

Jessie closed his eyes and dropped his head back against the couch. "You wouldn't be arguing if you could read my thoughts. I almost kissed you just then. You don't want that."

Theo's gaze snapped to Jessie's lips. The instant longing stole the air from his lungs. Before Theo could stop himself, he moved. His lips touched the corner of Jessie's mouth. His bravery fled the moment his lips met Jessie's skin. Theo immediately pulled away. "There. Now I'm the guilty one. You don't need to think about my age any long—" Jessie's mouth claimed Theo's, cutting off his words. The desire was instant and crippling. Logically, Theo knew Jessie was high and likely didn't know what he was doing. Not only would he not remember this, he probably would never kiss Theo sober. In a way, that was freeing. Theo could touch him and kiss him without blushing tomorrow. It was like a free pass. Their tongues stroked. Theo's cock stirred. Lust had his entire body pulsing. Jessie came at him so hard that Theo half expected to get fucked. Then it was over. Jessie sat up and clasped his head.

"Damn. The room is spinning."

Theo scooted over and urged Jessie down. "Come on, sweetie. Put your head in my lap and close your eyes. It'll pass. I've got you."

Doing as told, Jessie curled onto his side with his head on Theo's lap. Theo ran his fingers through Jessie's hair over and over until he felt Jessie go limp. Theo held his breath and checked Jessie's pulse. His heartbeat felt steady. Theo went back to stroking his hair and shoulder. He stole his chance to rub Jessie's cut bicep. The door opened and Declan stepped inside. He looked their way. Theo flashed the guy a small smile. With a nod, Declan toed off his shoes and locked up. He set the alarm before joining Theo. Theo went back to running his fingers through Jessie's hair while Declan filled the chair beside him. Declan eyed Jessie, looking worried. Theo flashed him another reassuring smile.

"He's still breathing."

Declan nodded, as if that was all he needed to know.

They sat in the silence for several minutes. Theo kept stroking Jessie and tried to work up the nerve to talk to Declan. While Declan was like everyone there—nice—Theo didn't want to overstep. Unfortunately, his curiosity always got him in trouble and his need to know was already out of control. Theo couldn't take it anymore.

"May I ask you something?"

Declan's hands lifted and fell. "Don't ask what he's on. Something to pick him up. Something else to bring him down. One thing because he can't sleep and another because he can't stay awake. One thing to get him through the day. Something else to help him forget. I gave up trying to keep up a long time ago."

Theo dropped his gaze to Jessie. He looked so

peaceful in Theo's lap. Theo wasn't dumb. He knew Jessie wasn't in a normal sleep. He was unconscious. That was why Theo hadn't left. He was scared Jessie would stop breathing if he stopped touching him. Theo shook his head as he met Declan's stare again.

"I wasn't going to ask that. Half the guys in my group home were always strung out on something. This is just another night for me. I was wondering how long you've been in love with Ezra."

To Theo's surprise, a low rumble of laughter cut through the air. Declan's eyes swam with humor as he glanced Theo's way. Theo fully expected a denial to follow. Instead, Declan kept surprising him.

"Hmm, well. Always, I suppose." Before Theo could ask, Declan leaned his head back and sighed loudly—like relieved to have the truth off his chest. He eyed Theo for a moment and smiled. "I used to have this dog—Lucifer." Theo didn't know what that had to do with anything, but he stayed quiet and listened anyhow. "Lucifer was a huge Rottweiler and aptly named. That dog was Satan when it came to anyone but me. Everyone was scared of him. I worried all the time that Jessie would make me get rid of him. Then Jessie and Ezra's mom passed away and Ezra moved in here." Another soft chuckle escaped Declan—like he couldn't resist whatever memory he saw inside his head.

"Lucifer and I were both immediately overprotective of him. He looked so angelic and fragile. Lucifer followed Ezra everywhere he went like a lovesick puppy. Ezra bought him a pink tutu to wear and it was like that poofy skirt changed Lucifer's entire personality. Suddenly, everyone wanted to pet him, and Lucifer ate it up." Declan's smile slipped away. "Then, a few years later, Lucifer had a stroke. He lost the ability to swallow, so the vet said the kindest thing I could do would be to put him to sleep. I was devastated. He was my baby. Ezra sat with him so I wouldn't have to watch Lucifer die, but he wouldn't be alone. Then he stayed up with me all night so I wouldn't be alone either. He made sure I ate and never once treated me like I was an idiot for grieving so hard over a pet. Ezra was holding my hand and rubbing my arm. I looked over and it was like all my denials were ripped away. All that overprotectiveness showed its true face." Declan snorted and shook his head. "It's not like I'm blind. I've always known that Ezra is extremely beautiful on the outside." Declan met and held Theo's stare. "But that's nothing compared to how heart-stoppingly gorgeous he is on the inside. I've known him all his life. Do you have any idea how completely fucked up that is?"

Theo lifted one shoulder in a half shrug. "Lots of people fall in love with people they've known their whole lives. You're both adults. It's none of my business, but you should tell him. Not everyone gets lucky enough to find love."

Declan snorted. "I'm not the type to burn bridges while I'm fucking living on them. Even if, and this is a big if, even if he said he felt the same, I still work for his brother. His very protective brother who has been more like a father to Ezra. Losing this job, this family I've chosen for myself, that's not an option for me."

"So... what? Do you plan to watch Ezra eventually fall in love with someone else and have a life elsewhere?"

A heartbreaking smile touched Declan's lips. "That's exactly what I plan to do." Declan sat forward and eyed Jessie. "I think he'll live through the night. He looks peaceful. Would you like me to carry him to bed before he wakes up and pukes in your lap?"

Theo dropped his gaze to Jessie. His hair was soft. Theo couldn't stop touching him. He didn't know how to give up the human contact he craved so much. "No. I'm good. If you take him to bed, I'll worry about him all night."

Declan shook his head and stood. "Good luck to you, then. You'll never sleep again if you plan to always worry about him."

"I thought you cared about him." The words burst from Theo with no permission from his brain. He didn't like sounding like a dick, but Declan sounded like he had given up on Jessie.

A sad smile briefly crossed Declan's features. He shook his head. "You're a nice person, Theo. I can tell you already care a lot about Jessie. So it would be cruel for me to be anything less than one hundred percent honest with you. Jessie is fucked up. He has been fucked up for a very long time and he likely isn't long for this world. Some people—no matter how good they are in their heart—they are only meant to burn bright and hot until they fade away. Jessie is so massively talented that it's blinding, but he doesn't know how to be anything else. Just don't expect too much, okay?"

Theo didn't even need to think about Declan's warning. "I don't expect anything at all." He really didn't. Declan didn't know him. No one had ever loved him or wanted him. Jessie had already given him more than anyone else ever had. Every day was just icing at this point.

Declan nodded. "I know and yet Jessie will still probably break your heart. If you decide you want me to carry him down the hall, just call my cell. I don't really sleep anyhow."

"Okay. Goodnight."

With a nod, Declan started away before stopping and focusing on Theo once more. "By the way, thank you for asking about Ezra. No one ever does." Before Theo could think of a way to respond, Declan disappeared down the hall.

With a shake of his head, Theo went back to staring at Jessie. He traced the shell of Jessie's ear and then tucked his hair behind it. "What a strange group you all are. I've never seen a house so filled with love that no one acknowledges. How sad." Luckily for them, Theo had tons of love too and no one to share it with. He would add his to the mix. Maybe the weight of his affection would be enough to finally have everyone speaking their minds. He could hope. Theo smiled at the dream. One day, someone would love him too. When that day came, Theo swore he wouldn't be silent. In fact, he might never shut up again.

FIVE

Jessie couldn't stay away from Theo. He found himself arranging his entire day around the guy. First, they worked on getting him set up with a doctor in L.A. Then Jessie taught Theo how to drive and helped him get his license. The more he watched Theo grow, the more Jessie wanted to be a part of every aspect of his life. Considering the way everyone left them alone a majority of the time, Theo seemed to be the only one who didn't realize Jessie was falling sickeningly in love with Theo.

As per what was becoming habit, everyone made themselves scarce after dinner, leaving Jessie to have Theo to himself.

Theo eyed the empty kitchen. "Declan decided to go out again, I take it."

Jessie nodded. His head felt a little loose on his shoulders. He had admittedly taken a bit too many pills today. It was the only way he could deal with being alone with Theo and not pouncing. At least, that was what he was telling himself these days. "It's just you and me. What would you like to do?"

Theo shrugged. "You haven't been in your studio for a while. I could listen to you play or we could watch a movie."

"Let's watch a movie." That way, he could hold Theo on the couch.

"Lead the way," Theo said, motioning in the direction of the theater room. "You get to pick this time."

"That's cool. I'm good at picking stuff."

The way Theo smiled made the idiotic claim worthwhile. Jessie waited for Theo to sit so he could fill the spot beside him, sitting as close as possible. With the lights off, he fumbled with the remote before firing the huge screen to life. He searched genres and picked a horror movie. The moment the opening scene began, Jessie draped his arm across Theo's shoulders and settled in. At first, Theo felt stiff in his hold. After a few minutes passed, Jessie felt Theo relax. A few minutes more and Theo's hand moved to rest on Jessie's thigh. Jessie made it five minutes longer before he found himself reclining the loveseat and tugging Theo onto his lap so he could hold him properly. He swore he meant to stop there. For a few minutes, he genuinely tried to behave. But then his lips skimmed Theo's shoulder. Theo felt too damn good with his back settled against Jessie's chest and ass resting in the perfect spot. They had been spending too much time together. The desire had grown too big.

Jessie's arms tightened around Theo. He tried to make himself stop, but reality got a little harder to hold on to by the second. Jessie didn't imagine he would hold on to consciousness much longer and he wanted to touch Theo. His lips moved to Theo's neck. Jessie's tongue shot out. Theo squirmed in Jessie's lap. The air thickened. Jessie's hand moved without thought. The tips of his fingers slipped inside the waistband of the thin workout shorts Theo wore. Jessie's teeth sank into Theo's neck in a light nip. Theo whimpered. Jessie lost the ability to breathe properly. He had to know if Theo was hard for him. Jessie shoved his hand inside Theo's shorts. A breath that sounded ragged even to his ears burst from him when he found Theo not only hard but leaking. He didn't know anything but desire in that moment. With one hand cupping Theo's throat and the other massaging Theo's dick, Jessie sucked and licked Theo's neck and shoulder—like he wouldn't be forced to answer for this later. Theo squirmed in his lap, writhing against Jessie's palm. The room spun and Jessie leaned his head back and closed his eyes. He kept playing, feeling up Theo's balls and toying with his cock. Theo was so hard yet so soft and the different textures were feeding Jessie's high. Jessie felt good—like he floated on a cloud with a weighted blanket draped over him. His body grew heavier until he couldn't feel a thing and darkness swallowed him.

Theo's entire body was on fire. He didn't understand how it happened. One moment, he had been trying to work up the nerve to set his hand on Jessie's thigh. The next, he was in Jessie's arms getting pleasured. He was half a second away from blowing in Jessie's hand when Jessie went limp. Theo's first reaction was fear. He scrambled to check Jessie for a pulse. When he found Jessie's heart beating steady, the aggravation hit. He was so close. So fucking close. His cock twitched, begging for more pets. Theo couldn't ignore it. He was too close to the edge.

Theo slipped from the couch and rushed to his room. With the door locked and shut behind him, Theo shoved down his shorts and fisted his cock. He closed his eyes and tried clinging to the wisps of Jessie's touch. Damn, he wanted Jessie so much, it physically hurt. He stroked and squeezed while picturing Jessie doing the same. With one hand braced against the closed door, Theo leaned into it, stroking and thrusting against his palm. Pressure climbed his erection and beat against his crown. Theo pumped hard and fast, racing toward release. His muscles tensed. Theo held his breath. A loud gasp burst from his lungs as cum shot from his dick and nearly buckled his knees. Jessie's name rang out in his mind. Theo's eyes stung. He wanted to coat Jessie's body in his cum. Theo wanted Jessie to kiss him while sober and lucid—when he would remember doing it. He wanted Jessie to come to bed with him willingly and openly. Without shame. Theo wanted to be kissed in the morning when Jessie's eyes were clear of chemical influences. He craved being special. Loved.

Theo stared at the mess he had made and sucked air. He felt empty. Theo wasn't stupid. He knew

Jessie would never touch him sober. It was only when Jessie was out of his head and could no longer distinguish one body from another that he wanted Theo. Theo wasn't special; he was convenient. The saddest part of this was that Theo didn't care. Tomorrow night, he would patiently wait for Jessie's guard to drop again. He would be at the ready to be touched. That was how far he had fallen when it came to Jessie. Theo would take Jessie's inebriated caresses over a sober man's hands any day. Even high, Jessie was the one Theo wanted. Theo already knew that probably wouldn't change. He was as he had always been—pathetic.

SIX

THERE HAD BEEN ANOTHER BLOND SNEAKING away from the bedroom next door when Theo tried to leave his room. That was why Theo spent the day hiding. He was licking his wounds. Theo was hurt and humiliated. Each time he thought about racing back to his room to jerk off, he wanted to die. Sometimes, he wondered if Jessie faked unconsciousness to get rid of Theo so he could call up some experienced regular to fuck him. Theo was tired of being this way. He was exhausted with his innocence and his fragile heart. He wanted to be confident and sexy. Theo wished he could storm Jessie's bedroom and demand he be the one Jessie took to bed. His blood boiled at the idea of another goddamn person sharing Jessie's body. It was bullshit. Theo was right here, silently loving him.

It wasn't until the sky darkened and Theo's stomach growled in protest that Theo ventured from his room. The house was eerily silent. Theo stood at the counter and ate a sandwich in the otherwise empty kitchen while trying not to think. Unfortunately, the longer he stood there, the less he wanted to be alone. Fucking Jessie. Theo was too levelheaded when it came to him. He realized they weren't together. Jessie didn't owe him anything. They weren't a couple. Jessie had already given him more than anyone else alive. Theo needed to be happy with that and stop expecting Jessie to fall in love. Hell, Theo didn't have anything to offer. He was no prize. Jessie had taken him in and given him everything. Theo needed to suck it up and recognize Jessie would never be his. The man was too far above him.

With that depressing thought, Theo's appetite fled. He set his half-eaten sandwich aside and wiped his hands on his pants. Johnny—a nightshift guard Theo rarely saw—came through the door. He flashed Theo a smile on his way to the fridge. As Theo looked on, he grabbed a bottle of water and a small bag of peanuts they kept on hand just for him. As he headed back toward the door, Theo broke.

"Have you seen Jessie?"

Johnny paused at the question. He pushed his long blond hair out of his eyes as his light brown eyes moved Theo's way. "Yeah. About an hour ago. He was working in his studio."

Theo smiled. "Thank you."

With a nod, he headed back out, leaving Theo alone.

Theo took a breath. He needed to get over this. There was no time like the present. He headed for the studio. As he neared, Theo expected to hear music pouring out of the open door, but only silence met him. His steps slowed. He peeked inside. Jessie sat on the floor with two empty whiskey bottles and a half full one opened at his hip. Theo rapped his knuckles lightly on the door, announcing his presence.

Jessie's chin jerked up from whatever he was looking at on the papers in his lap. A sweet smile touched his lips at the sight of Theo. "Hey, baby. Where you been all day?"

Theo fought a wince. "Hanging out by myself."

Jessie visibly swallowed. "Did I do something to upset you?"

Theo's feelings immediately stopped mattering. He rushed to join Jessie on the floor. "No. Not at all. I was just having a pity party. You know, playing around online and trying to figure out my future."

A deep line appeared between Jessie's eyebrows. "Are you unhappy here with me?"

Jessie sounded so adorably hurt that Theo forgot every reason he had avoided him. "I'm very happy here, but I know I can't stay here forever. Eventually, I'll have to make my own way. I don't know how to do that. Honestly, I don't know how to do anything." The depression was back with that confession. He shook his head, hoping to shake off another bout of depression. "What are you working on?"

Jessie pulled a pained face. "I was trying to write a new song. A lot of words are flowing, but they aren't forming what I need."

"You write songs too?" Theo never stopped being blown away by Jessie. He was the brightly burning star that Declan accused him of being. His talent was blinding.

Jessie nodded. "I wrote all the songs and music for Malice Abyss. Songs used to just flow from me onto paper. Honestly, I've made more money from songwriting than anything. Now, there's nothing in my brain. I'm empty."

Theo's throat nearly swelled closed at the way Jessie proclaimed his emptiness. His words felt deeper than just no songs flowing—like he was dead inside. Theo crossed his legs and settled in. He couldn't let Jessie feel this way alone. "Tell me how I can help. How can I inspire you?"

Jessie took a swig from his open bottle as he stared at Theo. Theo's skin tightened at the heat in his stare. His intensity had chills running down Theo's spine. He felt wanted. Jessie had never looked at him like this, so directly. His kisses usually came in a sneak attack. This was different. This was how Jessie looked at people before he fucked them. Theo felt that all the way to his soul. "Tell me how you like to get fucked. Spare no details."

The breath left Theo. Jessie's words were an instant inferno, burning Theo alive. His mouth went dry. The truth slipped out while his brain was otherwise occupied. "I wouldn't know. I'm a virgin."

Jessie blinked. His entire demeanor shifted. Theo swore he heard a door inside Jessie slam against him, making it even harder for Theo to breathe.

When he didn't respond, Theo's nerves set in. He rubbed his hands on his thighs and licked his rapidly drying lips. "You could always change that, though. I imagine, in your years of fame, you've probably slept with thousands of people."

"That's a bit extreme," Jessie said, breaking his silence.

Theo ignored Jessie's interjection. "What I meant is, you probably have a ridiculous amount of experience." God help him. Theo couldn't stop. Jessie had snapped his brain by finally looking at him like he wanted to fuck him. "You could ease me into things, or whatever." By the time Theo finished his barely comprehensible babbling, Jessie looked extremely sober and closed to any suggestions from Theo.

"No."

Theo fought a wince. The sting of rejection made it hard to breathe. It was a familiar feeling for Theo. "Okay. I guess..." Theo rubbed his thighs again, fighting an oncoming panic attack. The walls were closing in. "I guess Grindr it is," he said with a forced laugh. Theo jumped to his feet. "I'm going to head back to my room and jump back on the internet. Gotta figure out my life, you know, and you need to get back to work."

"Don't you dare download that app, Theo. Stay here with me."

No matter how hard he tried, Theo couldn't

meet Jessie's gaze. He forced a carefree smile to his face that was so brittle, Theo scared himself. "Don't worry about me. It was a dumb idea. You would never want someone like me. I'm just a charity case you took in. I'm nobody at all."

"Theo." Jessie sounded exasperated.

Theo headed for the door without looking back. He already felt like a dumbass who had overstayed his welcome. Theo would never be able to look Jessie in the eye again after tonight. He felt like a goddamn loser. He was, but fuck. Jessie would sleep with anyone and everyone but him. Theo would always be Jessie's rescue pet. While Theo would always be grateful for everything Jessie had done for him, he couldn't spend another night under Jessie's roof. He couldn't handle the longing and unrequited ache in his gut. Maybe he was dumb as hell, but Theo was in love with Jessie. Jessie would never feel the same. The biggest way Theo could show his appreciation for everything Jessie had done for him was to get out of his hair. So Theo would set him free.

The moment he was back inside his room, Theo locked the door and got to work. He had lived on the streets once. Theo could do it again. He quickly changed clothes, dressing warm enough for a night under the stars. Theo didn't want to take any of the things Jessie had given him, but he couldn't completely avoid it. He would leave the expensive stuff. The laptop and phone. His necklace. Only the clothes on his back and what toiletries he could fit in his backpack would come along for the ride. If Theo ever got settled and found a job, he would send Jessie some money for the clothes. With nothing left to do, Theo turned in a slow circle and eyed the beautiful life Jessie had given him. His throat swelled. This place hadn't been free. It had cost him his heart and soul. Those had been the only things Theo had left when Jessie rescued him. Now he had nothing.

Theo took a breath. He had nothing left to lose, then. Theo headed for the window. He couldn't go out the door and risk being seen. If anyone stopped him and called for Jessie, Theo might not stand against Jessie asking him to stay. He couldn't do that. Theo wouldn't survive another morning of seeing a different guy leaving Jessie's room. After a cursory glance, Theo pried open the window. It was only a short drop. He easily climbed out. Since he didn't want anyone else coming in behind him, Theo worked at closing the window before taking off. He stuck to the shadows—the way he had done coming onto the property that first night. There was a tall fence along the line of Jessie's property, but the black metal bars were wide enough for someone starved to squeeze through. Jessie had been feeding Theo too good these past few months. He couldn't get through any longer. With no other options left to him, Theo followed the line of the fence until he reached the mouth of the driveway. The gates were open. Theo ran out. He made it half a mile before any cars passed. The first one that did immediately whipped to the side of the road. A groan rose in his throat. It was Ezra.

Ezra rolled down his window and waited.

Theo dropped his chin and sighed. There was no escaping this. He made his way to Ezra's side.

Ezra sat with his arms crossed and looking annoyed. "What are you doing?"

Theo's shoulders squared. "I'm leaving."

Ezra's hands fell to his lap. He stared up at Theo with hurt etching his features. "Why? I thought you cared about us."

Defeat washed over Theo. His eyes fell closed. "I love you a lot." Theo's voice cracked on the confession. His heartbreak was barely held in check. "You're my family, but I can't stay here anymore."

For a moment, Ezra eyed him in silence. Theo swore in that moment he felt Ezra's understanding. "Where will you go?"

Theo smiled at Ezra's obvious concern. He was such a nice person. It was like Jessie and Ezra were two sides of the same coin. They had enough similar features that Theo couldn't say they were too different to be related. But really, they were nothing alike. Theo shrugged. "I've lived on the streets before. It's no big deal for me to go back."

Ezra shook his head. His features hardened as much as someone as sweet as him could pull off. "Nope. I'm not having it. You're family now. Let's go back and grab the rest of your things. You'll stay with me."

Theo swallowed. He wanted away from Jessie. Ezra wasn't away from Jessie. "I don't have anything else. Even the clothes I'm wearing are Jessie's. Don't worry about me."

A loud snort escaped Ezra. The sound didn't suit him. "Please. Jessie wouldn't be caught dead in anything you're wearing. No offense. It's just not his style. Everything he owns is black. Plus, you're nowhere near the same size."

Theo thought of the stacks and stacks of clothing Jessie had given him. Confusion had his brow furrowing. "But where did all these clothes come from if they're not Jessie's?"

"Wherever Jessie sent Declan to buy them, I imagine. Now get in the car."

Theo's heart squeezed as he circled the car and slid into the passenger seat. Jessie had been taking care of Theo from the first moment they met. Theo had let it go on, losing more of himself every day to Jessie while Jessie remained untouched. It was a blow.

Thankfully, Ezra didn't speak. Low and slow music poured from the speakers. Ezra seemed to be lost in his own well of sadness. By the time they made it to Ezra's, Theo's chest felt so heavy, he thought he might suffocate. Theo climbed from the car, feeling like his legs were encased in concrete. While he had been to Ezra's so Declan could pick him up, Theo had never been inside. It was a nice place, but nothing compared to Jessie's. He didn't imagine Ezra needed anywhere near the space Jessie did. As they stepped inside, a sweet smell washed over Theo. The place smelled like Ezra's home. The thought made Theo smile despite his situation.

Ezra tossed his keys on the coffee table and motioned at the living room in general. "Welcome home."

Theo took it in. The place was immaculately decorated, which didn't surprise Theo at all. The couch looked soft and welcoming. Theo crossed the room and sat. The brown masterpiece cradled Theo's body. He almost sighed. "This is a nice place."

Ezra smiled as he sank into the spot next to Theo. He didn't turn on the TV or any lights. For several minutes, they sat in silence, lost in their thoughts. Ezra finally spoke, cutting through the pain slowly drowning Theo.

"Do you want to tell me why you left Jessie's? Did he do something?" Ezra made a dismissive motion before Theo could answer. "It's Jessie, so I know he did something, but what happened?"

Heat filled Theo's cheeks. He turned his head Ezra's way, but he had a hard time meeting Ezra's gaze. Theo swiped his hands on his thighs. "It's kind of embarrassing."

Ezra clucked his tongue. "Sweetie, some strange guy waxed my butt crack today in a room filled with makeup artists so I would be perfect for a photo shoot. I know humiliation. You can tell me anything."

Despite his best efforts, Theo couldn't stop blushing. He could hardly refuse to tell Ezra everything after Ezra admitted such a horrifying thing. "Um." Theo scratched his nose and focused on a spot across the room. "I asked Jessie to be my first and he refused." Theo said the words fast—like ripping off a bandage.

Ezra didn't as much as blink. "Your first what?"

Theo had never wished so hard for the floor to open and swallow him whole. "You know. My first... sexually."

The way Ezra blinked fast said a lot about how hard Ezra fought to keep his thoughts to himself. "Why?" Theo never dreamed he would have to explain himself. Thankfully, Ezra didn't force Theo to scramble for an answer before pressing on. "I mean, honestly, I love my brother, but he's probably slept with everyone on the planet except you and me."

Since Ezra calmly spoke, as if they were talking about the weather, Theo found himself relaxing and speaking just as freely. "That was sort of part of it—like I have no experience. None. I mean, I was raised in a group home and moved from there to being homeless. Never in my life have I been considered a catch. Truthfully, I'm a bit uncomfortable with being touched at all, even though I obviously want to be touched. I guess I thought, since he had likely slept with everyone, that he would be the best person to kind of ease me into things." Plus, Theo was so in love with Jessie that he died a little more every day. He couldn't admit that to Jessie's brother.

Ezra leaned his way and patted his knee. "Oh, sweetie. That's heartbreaking."

"Great." Theo didn't mean to sound quite so bitter, but Ezra was beautiful. In fact, his image likely showed up first online when anyone searched for beautiful men.

"I'll do it."

Theo's gaze snapped to Ezra's. "What?"

Ezra shrugged, as if sex meant nothing. "I'll be your first."

For a moment, Theo couldn't stop rapidly blinking. He imagined he looked the same as Ezra had earlier. "Um. Well. I imagine there isn't a single person on the planet who would say no to that offer, but I think I have to be the first. Declan has been beyond nice to me and he's super, super in love with you. I would feel like a horrible bastard if I slept with you." Plus, once again, Theo was in love with Ezra's brother.

Ezra stared at Theo like he had grown a second head. "What are you talking about? Declan isn't in love with me. He thinks of me as a little brother."

A loud and obnoxious cackle burst from Theo. Ezra didn't laugh. Theo's smile slipped away as the truth sank in. "Oh my god. You're serious." Theo couldn't wrap his mind around it. "Ezra? He is like sick in love with you. Trust me. No one has ever loved me. I can recognize the signs from miles away. He practically vibrates with hope and longing when you're around."

"Huh." Ezra spent a moment staring at nothing. "Well, that's... huh."

Theo decided to have mercy on him. "Thank you for the offer, though. I think I'm just doomed to be unwanted."

An adorable hint of irritation crossed Ezra's features. He stood. "Well, fluff all that. Come on."

Theo didn't move right away. "Where?"

A mischievous smile touched Ezra's lips. "I'm about to show you the power of your sexiness."

"I'm not sexy," Theo said automatically.

Ezra snorted. "Idiot. Come on."

With no other choice left to him, Theo followed Ezra down the hall. Ezra paused in a darkened doorway and switched on the lights before leading Theo into what appeared to be his dressing room. Theo didn't know how else to describe the space. There were bright lights surrounding a huge mirror with a salon-style chair parked in front. Makeup littered a long counter between the chair and mirror. Racks upon racks of clothing lined the room.

Ezra moved deeper into the room and patted the back of the chair. "Have a seat."

Theo didn't hesitate. Once he was seated, Ezra eyed the items scattered across the counter. He grabbed some tweezers before touching Theo's chin and turning his face from side to side, as if studying his lines. He went to work, plucking precise hairs and making Theo's eyes water. Theo didn't complain, even though he wasn't loving this. Thankfully, Ezra set the tweezers aside and grabbed some eyeliner.

"Don't worry. I'm not doing much. You won't look like you're wearing anything. I'm just making some subtle highlights. You have beautiful eyes. They can't be missed, but I can make men incapable of looking anywhere else."

Theo would have nodded, but he was afraid he would lose an eye.

"There," Ezra said, leaning away after tracing Theo's eyes. He grabbed a squirt bottle and lightly wet Theo's hair. He combed and swept Theo's hair from side to side, eyeing him before grabbing a pair of scissors.

"Um... don't you need to be licensed to do this or something?"

Ezra's gaze stayed locked on his task as he answered. "I'll pretend you didn't say that to me so we can stay friends, especially since you already turned down sex with me tonight."

Theo winced. "Sorry. I would never want to hurt you the way it hurt me when Jessie said no."

Ezra clucked his tongue. "My feelings aren't hurt. I get shot down all the time."

"No way," Theo said with a snort.

"Yes way." Ezra combed Theo's hair as he spoke. "Everyone thinks I'm too sweet. I'm not what's in style sexually. Everyone wants someone who likes to get beaten and choked or whatever. I'm everyone's little brother."

"You're marriage material."

Ezra froze at Theo's claim. Theo watched him as he turned inside himself. Ezra smiled. It was as sweet as him. "I like that. That sounds so much better than the truth. I'm boring. Thank you." Ezra didn't give him time to respond. He snipped the finest bit of hair and then went back to styling. Ezra added a touch of product and then stepped back. He smiled. "There. You've always been beautiful, but I took away a bit of the innocence."

Theo's gaze slid toward the mirror. Truly, he looked like a different person. He looked like he belonged in LA with all the beautiful people.

"Now," Ezra said, pulling Theo to his feet. "Let's make it look like you're relaxed in your beauty." With Theo on his feet, Ezra brushed at his shirt, as if making sure no stray hairs lingered before he turned toward the racks of clothes. He found a soft-looking blue flannel shirt and had Theo put it on over his t-shirt. "Leave it unbuttoned," Ezra ordered as he went to work rolling Theo's sleeves up to the elbow. With that out of the way, Ezra scrunched the material in a few places, making it look like Theo had been wearing it all night. He stepped back and eyed Theo. A small smile touched his lips as his gaze met Theo's. "Perfect. Let's go."

Theo followed Ezra without argument. Ezra looked determined and Theo needed someone to take charge right now. Otherwise, he might beg Ezra to take him back to Jessie. They climbed back inside Ezra's car and drove down the street to a nondescript brick building. It was definitely a short enough distance they could have walked, but Jessie didn't complain. He was still just along for the ride. As Theo slipped from the car, he spotted a lit neon sign above the red door: The Back Porch.

Ezra glanced his way as they headed for the door. "Gird your loins. Your virginity is very much in danger here."

Theo's forehead furrowed. "In a place called The Back Porch?"

Even though it hadn't been a question, Ezra treated it as one. "Yes. If anyone asks to speak to you in private, say no. That's how they sneak into your pants here."

"Okay. Loins girded. No private chats."

With a sharp nod and looking more serious than Theo had ever seen him, Ezra opened the door and waved Theo inside. It was a coffeehouse. Theo wasn't sure what he had been expecting, but a brightly lit cafe wasn't it. Heads turned their way as they stepped inside. A sexy guy in his mid-twenties, wearing ripped jeans and a smile, headed their way. He was huge—like a linebacker—but his smile was sweet and totally for Ezra. Theo watched him pull Ezra into a hug, swallowing him whole.

"I want you to meet my friend," Ezra said, his voice muffled by a massive chest.

The guy pulled away and focused on Theo at Ezra's words. "All right." He tucked Ezra under his arm. "Who's your friend?"

Ezra motioned Theo's way. "Wrecker, this is

Theo. Theo, Wrecker. Wrecker owns The Back Porch."

Theo didn't hesitate to shake hands with him. Wrecker had light brown skin that made Theo look pale. His light eyes looked like a lion's eyes and fascinated Theo. Despite his awe, Theo held on to his manners. "It's nice to meet you."

"You too," Wrecker said before turning his gaze back Ezra's way. "Is this your dude?"

Humor flashed in Ezra's eyes. He gave Wrecker's stomach a pat. "Theo is too good for me. He belongs to Jessie."

Theo wanted to argue, but Wrecker's eyes latched on to Theo with a new appreciation. His expression stole Theo's breath.

"Fascinating. Well, let's get you guys a table. What'll it be tonight?"

Ezra answered for them. "Two no-cal white geishas, please?"

"You got it," Wrecker said as he got them settled at a table near the front counter.

The instant Wrecker was gone, two men appeared from nowhere as if summoned by demons. They were both dark haired, light eyed, and beautiful like everyone in LA. "May we buy you a drink?"

It took Theo a moment to realize they were both focused on him—like Ezra wasn't even there.

"Um..."

Wrecker reappeared carrying two coffees and hissing like an angry cat. "Begone, vultures. These two are my guests."

They cast Wrecker a pouting look before two heated gazes lingered on Theo. "We'll be over there," they said simultaneously, pointing toward a nearby table like they had practiced the move.

Wrecker flashed him a sexy smile. "You have to ignore some of these guys. They're always looking for fresh meat."

Theo's gaze moved Ezra's way in just enough time to catch the way he hid his smile behind his drink. He focused on Wrecker again. "This is a nice place."

"Thank you, I—"

"Could we get some service over here, please? God. We've been waiting forever."

Wrecker pinched the spot between his eyes. "Damn. I need some reliable help. Excuse me."

Theo picked up his coffee and eyed the room. There wasn't a single woman in sight, but several men who were obviously couples sat close. Others eyed the room, as if checking out the wares while some openly flirted. Theo had never been to a club, but this place seemed to be some low-key version of a nightclub.

"This is a place for people looking for company, but who don't like the party scene," Ezra explained, easing Theo's curiosity. "It's always pretty much the same people. Those guys who approached you are Remington and Roscoe. They're harmless. You've already met Wrecker. He's a big sweetie. You'll love him. Everyone is staring at you."

Wrecker reappeared before Theo could call him a liar. "So, Theo, I see you have at least one amazing friend. Are you looking for another?"

"Do you plan to wait on anyone else tonight, Wrecker?"

As another angry customer yelled at Wrecker, Theo saw the man's wide shoulders fall in defeat. Theo felt an ounce of pity rise to the surface. "If you need help, I'm not doing anything."

Wrecker looked like he was ready to drop. "If you're serious and need a job, you're hired. Be here tomorrow at five p.m., and the job is yours." He was off again before Theo could thank him.

When he met Ezra's stare again, Ezra looked satisfied. "There you go." A sad smile touched Ezra's lips, and—for the first time—Theo truly saw the unhappiness behind Ezra's beautiful mask. "When one man knocks you down, there's always another waiting to pick you up. Never forget that." Ezra set his cup aside. "Now you have a new place to live and a job. You're looking sexy AF. Men are eyeing you like their next meal. Are you ready to stop by Jessie's and tell him face to face you're leaving?"

A groan rose in Theo's throat. "Ugh. Do I have to?"

Ezra dug a bill from his pocket and tossed it on the table. "Yes. You have to. That's what big boys do. Don't worry. I'll be right there with you."

Theo fought the urge to pout as he stood. Ezra was right. Jessie had done way too much for Theo for Theo to be a little shit and run out on him without even telling him goodbye. It wouldn't be easy, but it was best he got all the heartbreak out of the way in one night. Tomorrow, he would come back here, go to work for Wrecker, and Theo would start a whole new life. Who knew? Maybe, one day, he would be the twink sneaking away from Jessie's bedroom without it breaking his heart. Crazier things had happened.

After waking up alone in the theater room, Jessie had spent the entire day champing at the bit and losing his mind with Theo locked in his room. Every horrible thought known to man had gone through Jessie's mind throughout the day. Had Jessie finally gone too far by passing out on Theo last night? Was Theo done with him now that he saw Jessie for the loser he was? Would he leave now? Finally, an idea had struck. Jessie would write Theo a song. He would show Theo how much he cared. Unfortunately, the longer he sat there, getting nowhere and obsessing over the many reasons Theo still hadn't come out of his room, the more he spiraled out of control. He didn't know anymore what he was doing. Then Theo had appeared. Jessie had sat with his knees pressed to Theo's and his belly full of liquor and pills. With lust pressing on his throat.

Now that Jessie had driven Theo from the room and broken the boy's heart, he spent all his time musing over life with Theo. It was funny how no matter how much he drank, snorted, or swallowed, Jessie still was never so far gone that he didn't recall every minute detail of each second he spent with Theo. He should have known Theo was a virgin. If Jessie was being honest with himself, he had known it in his heart. Jessie was paralyzed with self-loathing and thoughts of anyone else touching Theo. Sometimes, late at night, Jessie would kick back in Theo's bed while Theo read comic books to him, and he would dream. Occasionally, Jessie would have flashes of total belief that he could change. That he could be more for Theo. The darkness always won, though. His addictions always beat him.

Jessie had a little baggie filled with pills in his pocket. He didn't even know what they were anymore. Jessie shook all the pills out into his palm. The different colors swirled and mixed, promising freedom from his ghosts. They promised no more dead eyes would stare at him once the life left his own eyes. Jessie poured them into his mouth and then chugged what was left of the whiskey.

A small chuckle rose in his throat, choked away by an unexpected wave of tears. He fell backward and stared at the ceiling. No one understood what it was like to be him. If he wasn't creating music, the unhappiness suffocated him. Even if the music flowed from him, it had nowhere to go anymore. He was a one-man band now. Theo was somewhere else, checking out Grindr, and all Jessie's friends were dead. Declan stayed for Ezra's sake and Ezra only came around out of loyalty. On and on. The vicious cycle churned. Jessie was the only one who could make the wretched suffering stop. Remove him from the picture, and everyone else moved on.

Jessie's breathing shallowed. He swore he heard his heartbeat slow. Jessie closed his eyes. An image of Theo was there waiting. A tear slipped from the corner of Jessie's eye and rolled back into his hair. He hoped Theo met someone gentle. Someone kind. The world would be so much brighter once Jessie was gone.

THE HOUSE WAS DARK AND QUIET AS THEY CAME through the door. Ezra glanced around as he set his keys on the kitchen table. "Declan must be off tonight. It's almost like the place is empty."

A sense of foreboding washed over Theo. Jessie had been more messed up than usual earlier. He had seemed... off. "Shit." Theo took off running. The door to the studio still stood open. Theo skidded to a stop inside the doorway. Jessie was on his back in the same spot where Theo left him. Theo knew. Before he even reached Jessie's side and dropped to his knees, he knew.

Ezra was right on his heels. "What's wrong—oh my god, Theo. Is he breathing?"

Theo checked for a pulse. There was nothing. He still tried to check for any signs of breathing. Nothing. Panic set in. "Call nine-one-one," Theo yelled, hearing the hysteria in his own voice. Without thought, Theo started CPR. He had been required to keep a certification to keep his teacher's aide gig that let him out of one class every year throughout high school. Back then, it had just been about fucking off for an hour every day. Never in a million years would he have thought he would have to use the knowledge. No one told him how terrified he would be.

Theo could hear Ezra on the phone, but not a single word penetrated his brain. He just kept up the chest compressions. His gaze met Ezra's stare over Jessie's lifeless body. Tears flowed down Ezra's face. Something inside Theo flared to life. Jessie would not fucking die on his watch. It didn't matter that Jessie didn't love him. As long as Jessie lived, Theo could live with anything. Jessie needed to be in the world somewhere.

A group of paramedics burst in followed closely by Johnny. They forced Theo aside. Everyone kept trying to ask him questions, but nothing made sense.

He had tunnel vision. Theo didn't see anything but Jessie.

"We have a pulse. It's weak."

Theo's knees gave out. Thankfully, Johnny was there to catch him. There weren't enough bodyguards in the world to save him if Jessie didn't make it. Jessie was the only thing keeping him tied to this shit-filled world. He had to make it, or Theo wouldn't.

SEVEN

THEO HADN'T BUDGED FROM JESSIE'S SIDE ALL night. Nurses came and went. Doctors checked in and spoke quietly in the hall with Ezra. Theo didn't move. While he commandeered one side of the bed, Declan took the other. On the inside, Theo felt like he had cried all the tears until his throat was raw and his soul deflated. In reality, Theo's eyes were so dry, they burned. His skin was cold to the touch, but he felt nothing. Sometimes, Theo thought his soul had died years ago, and—for whatever reason—he just kept surviving without it.

After speaking with the doctor and learning Jessie should be fine, Ezra had gone home to get some rest. Hours passed and Theo didn't even move to go to the restroom. It was like his body had shut down. When Ezra showed back up, looking a little better, it hit Theo how bad his back hurt. Declan tried flying to his feet and giving up his chair to Ezra, but Ezra slid in behind him. As he set his hands on Declan's shoulders, Theo swore he saw the will slip from Declan's body. He visibly relaxed as Ezra lightly rubbed his shoulders. While Declan might have had Ezra's touch, Ezra's piercing hazel eyes were focused on Theo, pinning him in place.

"Has he woken up at all?"

Theo shook his head. "There's no change."

Declan jumped in, as if he couldn't control his need to please Ezra. "How are you holding up? Do you need anything? Did you eat?"

Ezra squeezed Declan's shoulders. "I'm good, sweetheart. How are you? You're probably exhausted. I'll send someone to relieve you," Ezra tacked on without waiting for Declan's answer.

Theo couldn't take the waiting any longer. His heart hurt too bad. "I'm going to find a vending machine. Does anyone need anything?"

Declan and Ezra shook their heads.

Theo's knees popped as he pushed to his feet. He winced as his body protested sitting in the same spot all night.

Ezra reached out, stopping Theo as he passed.

He held Theo's arm and gaze. "Thank you. I will never, ever be able to repay you for saving the only family I have left." Ezra's voice shook with the power of his words.

Theo gave him a sharp nod. He felt dead on the inside, but he still tried for a small smile. Ezra released him, freeing him from the moment. Theo practically leapt from the room in his need to get away from everyone's stare. He found Johnny posted outside Jessie's door. Theo kept moving. He couldn't talk to anyone else right now. At the first restroom he spotted, Theo dipped inside. He nearly gasped when he caught sight of his reflection. His eyes were red and looked crazed. They were also black—like someone had punched him. A second of confusion rocked him on his heels until he remembered Ezra had put eyeliner on him. While still functioning completely on autopilot, Theo washed his face and hands. He did his best to avoid his reflection after that. Back in the hallway, he stared at a set of vending machines, still not seeing a thing. His heart raced into his chest when someone touched his arm. It was Jessie's nurse.

She had a kind smile. "Come with me. We have snacks for patients. You can pick something from there."

Theo tried for a smile and failed. Thankfully, she didn't call him on it. He followed her, seeing nothing. He simply kept moving. An odd peace settled over him as he stared at the offered snacks. Nothing appealed to him, but they had water and peanuts. Johnny was likely exhausted too. He grabbed those and headed back. Theo held the items out to Johnny as he reached the man's side.

"Fuck yeah," Johnny breathed with a bright smile, reaching for the snacks. For some reason, Theo felt a little more human in that moment.

"Thank you for everything." Theo said the words fast and then jumped back inside Jessie's room before anyone showed him an ounce of kindness. He knew that would break him.

Theo froze in his tracks as he cleared the doorway. Jessie was sitting up and awake. He was also alone. His hair was a mess and there were dark circles beneath his eyes. Still, he looked beautiful to Theo. Theo glanced around. His stomach unexpectedly fluttered with nerves. Jessie had almost died. It seemed intimate to be here now. Personal. "Where did everyone go?"

Jessie's sexy whiskey-colored eyes never budged from Theo. "Declan took Ezra to get me some things from the house."

"Oh." Theo felt a bit stupid. He looked away. He should have been the one to go. At least, if he had gone, Jessie would be left with someone he cared about.

"I hear you saved me," Jessie said, bringing Theo's gaze back to him.

Theo's discomfort doubled. "I suppose."

Jessie sighed and plucked at his covers. "Well, I doubt I'll ever forgive you for that."

"What's that supposed to mean?"

Jessie stopped fidgeting and held Theo's stare. "Don't pretend I'm not a mess. I'm a washed up has been with a dozen addictions that don't matter because I never expected to live this long. No one would've been surprised to find me dead. Not even me. Do you see now why you shouldn't be wasting your virginity on me, babe? Find someone to love you and put you on a pedestal before you think about giving away something I don't even remember having. I'm not worth your time."

For a moment, Theo couldn't look away. He felt so stupid. He had truly believed Jessie wouldn't remember that. While he had known Jessie was a mess, Theo hadn't known Jessie wanted to die. He took a breath. Theo was tired. He didn't have the strength to save anyone the way Jessie had rescued him. Theo moved to Jessie's side and lowered the bed railing. Jessie's eyebrows rose, but he didn't argue as Theo sat down next to his hip. Without a word, Theo wrapped his arms around Jessie's neck and hugged him close. At first, Jessie didn't hug him back. Then his arms lifted. Once Jessie gave in, his arms tightened. Theo's throat swelled. He swore he could feel how badly Jessie needed someone to hug him. It was possible, outside of sexual encounters and crazed fans, no one touched Jessie. Theo understood that feeling. No one except Jessie ever touched him either.

When Jessie's arms fell away, Theo stood. He didn't meet Jessie's gaze as he pulled the railing back into place. Theo didn't think Jessie would fall out of bed or anything, but he didn't want to risk it. A huge part of Theo wanted to walk away and say nothing, but Theo couldn't. Instead, he gripped the railing and tried to make his brain work. No matter how hard he thought, nothing came out sounding intelligent. In the end, he simply stared at Jessie's knees and spoke from the heart with no plan.

"It would be easy for anyone to say that you should feel blessed. After all, you can afford to do whatever you want whenever you want. No doubt, you probably feel like you can't complain because you've lived a life that would be a dream come true for anyone. The thing is, though, I would've listened to anything you have to say. I guess I thought, since I felt like I could talk to you about anything—like the whole humiliating virginity thing—that you knew you could talk to me about anything too." A humorless laugh burst from Theo. "If anyone understands being absolutely, blindingly unhappy, it's me. I'm not sorry I saved you, because it would break my heart if you no longer existed in the world. Not because of your music or money. Just because of you. If you don't want to do this living thing anymore, I can't fault you for that. I'm sorry I believed you needed me or cared." Theo's eyes burned. He worried if he stayed any longer, he would embarrass himself even more than he already had with Jessie. "You don't have to think about me anymore."

"Theo, I didn't..."

Theo didn't stick around for Jessie to find a way to finish his thoughts. He knew Jessie had issues and needed all the love he could get, but people had been loving him for much longer than Theo had been around. It wasn't working. Theo had been soul-weary long before he ever met Jessie. He couldn't save him. Jessie didn't want to be saved. There was nothing here for Theo but heartache.

THE CLOCK TICKING ON THE WALL WAS SO goddamn loud. Jessie thought his head might explode if he had to listen to it much longer. He needed his phone. Theo probably didn't want to hear anything Jessie had to say, but he couldn't say nothing. It wasn't like Jessie didn't know he was toxic. Fuck. He had been fucking up his entire goddamn life. Theo needed to know that wasn't on him. His eyes... Jessie scrubbed his fingers through his hair and tugged. He didn't want to be like this. That hug. Jessie's eyes fell closed. Theo's hug had been filled with genuine love. Jessie had felt it warming his chest. No doubt Jessie had already poisoned Theo's mind. Tainted him. He would never love anyone again as purely as he loved Jessie, because that was what Jessie did. He destroyed people.

Ezra slipped back inside Jessie's room. He was all smiles, but Jessie could see the underlying exhaustion he tried hiding. No one was more tired than Jessie. He couldn't go home and leave himself.

"I brought you clean clothes and whatnot. I also found your phone." He set an overnight bag aside and then handed Jessie his phone. "How are you feeling?"

"Like death," Jessie said absently as he tried unlocking his phone. It immediately died. "Ugh." Jessie smacked the back of his head against the upright mattress. "It's fucking dead."

Ezra flinched. "Sorry. I didn't think to grab a charger. I'll call Declan and have him bring you one. Do you need anything else?"

Jessie tried tempering his voice. Ezra was an awesome human. He didn't deserve to have Jessie as a plague upon his life. "Yeah. Would you have Declan make sure Theo got home okay and has everything he needs? I doubt he had money for a cab, and he looked exhausted when he left here."

Ezra pulled a pained face. "Um, sweetie. Theo moved out yesterday."

Jessie fought to hide the fact that he couldn't breathe at all. "He can't afford to move out. We just now got his license, so he hasn't had time to find a job. Did he go back to the streets?" Jessie couldn't live with that. He couldn't handle knowing Theo was cold and hungry all because Jessie was a dumb bastard.

Something passed over Ezra's features. He almost looked guilty. "He's living with me."

For half a second, Jessie almost lashed out, but it was Ezra. If Theo couldn't stay with Jessie any longer, Ezra's would be Jessie's second choice for him. "I'll send you some money for his care."

Ezra rolled his eyes. "You already do too much for me. Having Theo at my place is no hardship. In fact, it might be fun. It's been a while since I had anyone to go places with me. Being alone gets old." Ezra moved to the closest chair and sat. "I overheard a couple of nurses chatting when I came in. It sounds like you should get to go home tonight when the doctor makes his second rounds. That should give you something to smile about."

Jessie knew Ezra wanted to move past the Theo thing—like he didn't know Jessie was a horrible bastard. That was the way Ezra dealt with everything the least bit controversial. He ignored it. Not that Jessie could judge. Jessie had never been good at faking it.

"I'm not going home."

Ezra's smile slipped. "What do you mean?"

Jessie held Ezra's stare so Ezra couldn't dodge this truth. "Please stop pretending like I'm okay."

Ezra's eyes fell closed for a moment. His chest

expanded on a deep breath before he opened them again. "How do you want me to act, Jessie? Because I have to say, anything short of pouncing on you and beating the pluck out of you for all the years of making me deal with this will be pretending on my part." Jessie didn't flinch or speak. He needed to hear Ezra's thoughts, and—apparently—Ezra had many, because he didn't stop sharing. "Do you want me to scream my throat raw? Would it make a difference? I love you. I have to pretend you're okay because you are all I have." Ezra's voice broke, shattering Jessie's heart.

Jessie couldn't keep doing this. "When they release me, I want to check in to rehab. Will you go with me?"

A tear slipped down Ezra's cheek. He nodded as he wiped it away. "Of course." A hint of a smile touched Ezra's lips. "I'm so proud of you."

Jessie wiped his sweaty palms on the sheet covering him. "Don't be proud of me yet. This might be a complete disaster."

Ezra stared at the opposite wall. A secretive-looking smile touched his face. "Oh, I don't know. You've never been in love before. I think you'll do everything in your power for him."

To Jessie's surprise, heat rushed to his cheeks. "I'm old enough to be his dad."

A snort escaped Ezra. It turned into a soft chortle before he burst into laughter. It had been so long since Jessie had seen Ezra laugh and mean it that—for the first time in ages—Jessie thought he might be okay. He would try. Not only did Ezra deserve to be set free from Jessie's problems, Ezra was right. Jessie loved Theo. He had to be whole for him. He had to heal for them.

EIGHT

Working for Wrecker made the time go by. It gave Theo a purpose. Made him put one foot in front of the other, even when he didn't want to anymore. Wrecker was quiet and steady. Peaceful. He was exactly the friend Theo needed after the tidal wave known as Jessie. Theo's gaze slid Wrecker's way. He washed, dried, and stacked coffee cups—like he had been doing it for years. The same as he had been doing every night since Theo started working for him four months ago. It was always just the two of them after closing every night. He had learned a lot about the guy since they had plenty of cleaning time every day to shoot the shit. Theo had learned his first thought about Wrecker was true. He had been a linebacker who played at a pro level. Coming out publicly as gay had tanked his career, but he had made enough money to open this coffeehouse. The Back Porch was known as somewhat of a haven for gay men. Wrecker took a lot of pride in the place and it showed. Theo liked him a lot. He let Theo be still. For someone whose life had always been loud and out of his control, Theo appreciated Wrecker more than the guy would ever know.

Wrecker turned and caught Theo watching him. A smile lit his face. He tossed his hand towel over his shoulder and headed Theo's way. "So do you have any big plans tonight?"

Theo shrugged. "Ezra wants me to go to Jessie's with him so he can give Declan his Christmas present. I plan to put up the Christmas tree while I'm there." He shrugged again, feeling exposed. "With Jessie coming home tomorrow, I hope decorating for him might make up for the fact that I won't be there."

Wrecker's forehead furrowed. "You know you don't have to work tomorrow. I could close the place alone."

"No. It's fine. I'd rather be here. I'm not family and Jessie and I didn't exactly part on the greatest of terms. It's better for me to be here. Ezra and Jessie need a quiet family Christmas."

Wrecker still looked worried. Theo had a bad feeling he didn't intend to let it go. "I know I don't say it enough, but truly, you've been a blessing. Everyone is always looking for a job here, but no one wants to work. You've been here every day and every holiday, pulling double shifts. You make me feel like shit sometimes—like I'm working you too hard. Tomorrow is Christmas. You already worked Thanksgiving."

Theo waved off Wrecker's concerns. "I don't have anyone except Ezra. Don't worry about me. At least, if I'm here, then I'm useful."

A loud huff escaped Wrecker. "You're always useful."

"Okay," Theo said with a smile, hoping to move past this. He headed for the back to grab a broom.

Wrecker was hot on his heels. "Seriously, Theo. Don't say 'okay' just to placate me. I think you're amazing. Say it with me. I'm amazing."

Theo grabbed the broom and headed back toward the front. He flashed Wrecker a laughing smile as he passed.

Wrecker wasn't having any of it. He followed

while Theo tried sweeping around him. "Come on, Theo. I want to hear the words. Say, I'm amazing."

"You're amazing," Theo chanted dutifully.

"Not me," Wrecker said, taking Theo's broom away and leaving Theo no other choice but to look at him.

Theo swallowed a sigh. "If I tell you I'm amazing, will you let me finish cleaning? Ezra will be here any minute to get me."

"I'll finish cleaning. Don't worry about that. Tell me one good thing about yourself and I'll let this go."

Theo forced himself to take Wrecker seriously. His throat swelled immediately. He couldn't think of a single thing. Theo was just existing at this point. No amount of meeting new people or avoiding the truth saved him from losing Jessie. Every time he closed his eyes, he saw Jessie's lifeless body on the floor again. Theo had told himself he would be good as long as Jessie was alive somewhere in the world. He had been granted his wish, so he would find a way to keep surviving. But Theo saw nothing good about himself. That was asking too much.

"No. Why is that in my coffeehouse?"

Wrecker's outrage shook Theo from his musings. He glanced behind him and found Ezra holding a tiny gray and white Pitbull puppy in a Christmas tutu.

Ezra didn't look the least bit chastised. "I couldn't leave Icarus in the car alone. He's a chewer." He bounced the dog up and down like a baby. His gaze latched on to Theo. "Are you ready? Johnny dragged out the tree and decorations for you and he's making Declan stay in his room so I can surprise him. He won't last long, though."

Theo glanced Wrecker's way.

Wrecker waved him toward the door. "Go. Get out of here. Enjoy your night."

Out of instinct, Theo hugged Wrecker and then quickly turned away. He felt a bit stupid, especially since Ezra wore a smile that screamed he thought something that wasn't true. Theo didn't have a thing for Wrecker. He loved Jessie. Always would. Most likely, one day, he would move on. Today wasn't that day, and Theo already knew the truth. He could move on, but no one would ever eclipse Jessie in Theo's heart. Everyone only got one first love. Jessie was Theo's. There was no changing that.

Ezra was a nervous wreck. Buying Declan a

new puppy was a huge risk. Declan might toss them out. If so, Ezra would take Icarus back home with him. That was no problem, but Ezra really wanted to make Declan smile. Declan and Ezra had an odd and complicated relationship. He had known the guy literally his entire life. Declan had been there, witnessing every high and low of Ezra's life. They loved each other. It was just... complicated.

Theo flashed him a reassuring smile that looked brittle to Ezra as they came through Jessie's back door. Ezra got it. He always felt the same mixture of emotions when he came here. Some beautiful memories lived under this roof. So too did some of the worst.

"You got this. Declan will love him." He scratched Icarus under his chin. "How could he not?"

Ezra took a bracing breath and nodded. "Here we go." Ezra headed down the hallway. At Declan's bedroom door, he paused and took another deep breath before knocking. "I'm coming in. I hope you're dressed." With that warning out of the way, Ezra pasted on his brightest smile and burst into the room. "Surprise. Merry Christmas."

Fudge. Declan wasn't fully clothed. In huge work boots and tight jeans, he stood shirtless, massive chest and rock-hard abs on display. He reached for a shirt as if intent on covering himself. Then he noticed Icarus and changed directions.

"Oh wow. Who are you?"

Ezra handed the blue-eyed puppy to Declan. "This is Icarus. He's been looking forward to meeting his new daddy."

The pure joy on Declan's face made Ezra's going out on a shaky limb worthwhile. Declan kissed the puppy's cheek, making loud kissy noises. "You're so adorable. This is amazing."

Ezra still felt a little shaky. He didn't want to disappoint Declan. "His food and everything else is in the kitchen. I brought everything he needs—leash, food, bed, and toys. He's also pretty much housebroken. I hoped he would make a good travel companion for your trip, but if you'd rather not take him just now, I can take him back home with me until you get back."

Declan eyed Icarus. "Nah. He looks like a good boy. Don't you, baby? Are you ready for a long car trip around the country?" Declan's gaze latched on to Ezra and didn't budge. "Thank you, angel. This is the best gift in the world."

Ezra fought to show any reaction. He wasn't ready to not see Declan for almost two months. It had always been hard to watch Declan leave for these yearly trips and go touring with Jessie. Ezra was always left behind. To stop himself from continuing to eyeball Declan's half nude body, Ezra cast a glance around the room. Declan's room was one of the biggest in the house. Jessie hadn't wanted Declan to feel the need to leave it if he needed space from working. One side looked like a normal bedroom—bed, dresser, nightstand, and closet. The other half looked like a small sitting room. Large chair, coffee table, entertainment center, and bathroom. Ezra headed that way. A box filled the chair. Ezra grabbed it and planned to simply move it to the table.

Declan set the dog on the floor. "Don't. I'll get that."

The box was much heavier than Ezra anticipated. He glanced down. A magazine on top caught his gaze, making him pause. Before the truth of what he was seeing sank in, the bottom gave out and magazines scattered, plopping onto the floor and sliding away. Ezra immediately dropped to his knees.

"Holy carp. I'm so sorry." He froze as he stared down at the mess. They were him. All of them were him. It looked to be every magazine Ezra had ever posed for, including the ones he hadn't thought

Declan or Jessie knew about. Ezra slowly shifted back to his feet. He turned in a slow circle, eyeing the mess. Declan went down onto one knee at Ezra's feet and started stacking the magazines into piles. He didn't meet Ezra's gaze. Ezra couldn't look at anything else. He stared a hole in Declan's head, willing him to look his way. Declan wouldn't. His motions got angrier by the second until he was slapping magazines together hard enough to send Icarus running for cover. Ezra touched Declan's shoulder. Declan froze but still didn't lift his head. Ezra moved closer until he could cup Declan's chin and force his head up. Still, Declan kept his gaze averted. On his knees, Declan still came to Ezra's chest. His lips were full and beautiful. Ezra had dreamed of them more times than he could count. He found himself stroking them now.

"Please don't," Declan whispered, sounding desperate.

Ezra couldn't stop. His heart was in control. He leaned down and kissed him. It was merely a sweet clinging of lips on lips with Declan's face clasped between his hands. Ezra's heartbeat pounded in his ears. His entire body gravitated toward Declan. No one had ever measured up to Declan in Ezra's eyes.

No one hurt him the way quietly loving Declan murdered Ezra.

"Please don't do this to me," Declan begged against Ezra's lips.

Tears filled Ezra's eyes at the plea. A lump formed in his throat. He hurt. Ezra always hurt. His hands fell away from Declan's face, setting him free. "You'll sleep with any little blond twink you can lure home, but you won't even kiss me."

Declan jerked back as if Ezra had slapped him. "Ezra, I—"

"Shut up, Declan." Ezra stepped around him and headed for the door. He had humiliated himself for the last time with Declan. Ezra got it. They would never happen. He was the only man on the planet Declan wouldn't touch. Ezra couldn't hang around here anymore, watching Declan sneak his whores from the house while Ezra acted like he didn't notice. Ezra's heart couldn't take this anymore. He was done.

WITH JOHNNY'S HELP, THEY HAD THE TREE upright and lit in no time. Theo only managed to hang a handful of ornaments before Ezra reappeared, head down and walking at a clipped pace. He was out the door, slamming it behind him before Theo could ask how things went. Theo tossed a questioning look Johnny's way.

Johnny shook his head. "You had best go after him. I'll finish this."

Theo wanted to run as fast as he could, but he also wanted Jessie to come home to a nice Christmas. "Are you sure?"

With his gaze locked on the tree, Johnny nodded. "Seriously. Go. All Declan does is make Ezra cry. At least, with you, he's not alone now."

With that tidbit of information lighting a fire beneath him, Theo raced after Ezra. He found him leaned against his car and swiping furiously at his eyes. Before Theo could ask what happened, Ezra spoke up.

"I need you to do something for me."

Theo didn't hesitate. "Okay. Anything."

"I need you to tell me I'm not fat and ugly."

"Um. Okay." Theo was confused as hell.

"Look, I know that you don't think I have any real problems, but I do. When push comes to shove, I can be the most self-destructive person you've ever seen. Right now, I'm half a second away from burning everything down that I have worked so hard to overcome because I'm feeling really fat and really ugly. So if even a small part of you thinks that I'm not fat and ugly, please tell me so before I lose myself again."

Theo closed the distance between them and gathered Ezra in his arms. He pressed his lips to Ezra's forehead. "You are the most beautiful man I have ever set eyes on, and if I hadn't—stupidly—fallen in love with your brother, you would be filing a restraining order against me right now."

A watery-sounding laugh burbled from Ezra. He clung tighter to Theo. "Why am I so dumb?"

Theo blew out a breath that sounded ragged, even to his ears. "I think you're brilliant."

Ezra dropped his chin and pressed his face to Theo's shoulder. Hot tears seeped through Theo's shirt. Ezra sniffed, sounding broken. "Thank you for not asking me what happened."

"You'd tell me if you felt like talking about it."

Ezra cried harder, ripping out Theo's heart. The open heartache he showed couldn't be faked. It was raw. Theo swore he could feel Ezra's heart breaking.

"Give me your keys, sweetie. I'll drive us home."

With a nod, Ezra dug his keys from his pocket and passed them Theo's way. Theo drew a steady breath as Ezra circled the car and climbed inside on the passenger side. He would take Ezra home and put him to bed, then maybe he would raid Ezra's liquor cabinet and get blind drunk. That was the only way to deal with such a bullshit-filled world where no one was treated like they deserved. Maybe Jessie had been right all along. Oblivion was the key to survival. This ugly world could suck his dick.

NINE

JESSIE COULDN'T RECALL THE LAST TIME HE FELT truly nervous, but he did now. Theo hadn't been to see him the entire time he was in rehab. Ezra had kept him updated with pictures he snapped of Theo on the sly. From what he understood, Theo still lived with Ezra and was doing great. He had a job and was saving money. Jessie couldn't wait to see him again. He wanted to see how much better Theo was for himself. While Jessie had been somewhat grateful for Theo not seeing him while Jessie had been suffering the worst withdrawals of his life, it was Christmas now. Jessie was home. Ezra would be here any minute. There was no way Theo could avoid Jessie tonight.

By the time Jessie heard Ezra coming through

the door, Jessie was swiping his sweaty palms on his thighs and was a half a second away from pacing. He swore his eyes itched with desperation to see Theo. Jessie flew to his feet the moment Ezra came into view. His heart fell when Ezra closed the door behind him. He was alone.

Jessie's throat swelled, but he still forced a smile to his lips. He crossed the room to relieve Ezra of his armful of presents and hug him. "There's my baby brother."

A bright smile lit Ezra's face. His eyes looked dull, though, making Jessie wonder exactly how long Ezra had been miserable and hiding it. "I'm so, so happy to see you. You look amazing." Ezra hugged him again with more strength than Jessie thought him capable of doing.

"You do too. Where's Theo?" Jessie couldn't hold the question inside. It burst from him, sounding every bit as desperate as he was.

Ezra didn't quite meet his gaze. "He had to work, but he sent a gift and asked me to tell you how proud he is of you."

Jessie waved off the words. "He's working? On Christmas night?"

Ezra peeled off his jacket. "You know how Wrecker is about holidays. He built The Back Porch for people to have a family of their choosing. It's a place for the displaced. That means being open on Christmas. Since Theo doesn't have any family, he volunteered to work tonight."

"Didn't he know I was coming home today?"

Ezra's smile looked a tad brittle. "Of course he did. Who do you think put up the Christmas tree? Theo came by last night, put up the tree, and made sure someone had stocked the fridge with your favorite foods."

Despite his best efforts to find some hope in Ezra's words, Jessie's heart sank. He had been telling himself the past four months that he would fix things with Theo once he was sober. It didn't sound like Theo had any desire to let Jessie make things right.

Ezra grabbed one of the gifts he brought and handed it to Jessie. "You need this. Don't be sad. Open his gift. I want to see your face."

Honestly, Jessie had wanted to open Theo's present alone. He had to admit he was excited, though. People didn't buy him gifts usually. He was the one who supported everyone else. Jessie didn't mind. He loved taking care of people, but this was incredibly sweet. It had been immaculately wrapped, as if Theo had taken great care to make it perfect. Jessie realized Ezra was right. He needed this. Jessie pried open the tape and slipped open the box. Inside was a shadow box filled with memories of them. There was a paper copy of Theo's driver's license. Receipts he had obviously snagged from restaurants after Jessie paid for dinner. A chuckle escaped Jessie as he spotted a happy-face sticker he had given Theo after seeing the doctor. He couldn't believe Theo had kept all these little mementos of their time together. There was even a gum wrapper that Jessie made into a flower for Theo. Jessie could barely breathe. He wanted to be with Theo so badly, it felt like withdrawals.

Ezra smiled and patted his knee. He stood and put his jacket back on. "Go. This is just another day, but you shouldn't spend another one without him. We can open gifts together anytime."

Jessie sniffed. Between Theo's gift and having such an amazing brother, Jessie was moved. A chuckle slipped from him. "You just want to run away before you're forced to face the consequences for bringing another dog into my house while I was gone."

"Yep. That's why I'm running," Ezra said with a bright smile. He gave Jessie another hug. "I really am so very, very proud of you and I want to spend some real time together soon. So go get your man. You both love each other too much to be stupid."

Jessie saluted him. "Yes, sir." As silly as he was being, it was all an act. The moment Ezra was gone, Jessie flew into action. His desperation was on full display and he shoved his feet in the first pair of shoes he could find. Once he had his shit together, he grabbed the gift he bought for Theo and headed out. Jessie mentally hit the ground running. He had to get his man.

THE CHRISTMAS CROWD WASN'T THICK AT THE Back Porch. Still, just like on Thanksgiving, Theo could see why Wrecker wanted to keep the place open. The people who trickled in were obviously searching for a way not to be alone. Even if they rarely spoke to each other, those who wandered in gravitated toward the other patrons, seeking human interaction. Theo fit in perfectly.

"Theo? Theodor Harlow?"

At the sound of his name, Theo's head shot up from wiping down the counter. A familiar set of light brown eyes were focused on Theo, waiting for his attention. An unexpected wave of rage washed over

Theo. He couldn't believe William stood there, saying Theo's full name—like he hadn't lured Theo to L.A. and then ignored his pleas for a place to stay.

"William." Theo didn't know what else to say. Even he heard the hatred in his voice.

Either William didn't hear it or he chose to ignore Theo's animosity, because his smile was bright. "Oh my god. I can't believe you made it here. How long have you been here?"

Theo held on to his temper by a thread. "Since the day you told me to meet you at the bus stop on Main and never showed."

William's smile faltered. "Honestly, I didn't think you'd find a way there, and I couldn't take off work on the small chance you might show."

As much as Theo wanted to scream that he had called every day on the long walk to L.A. and kept calling until his phone no longer worked when he got here, it wasn't worth it. William wasn't worth the time and effort anymore. "What can I..." The words died in Theo's throat as the door opened and Jessie stepped inside.

"Holy shit. That's Jessie Thunder."

William's words barely penetrated Theo's shock. Jessie looked ten steps beyond beautiful. Theo hadn't been prepared.

"Hello, gorgeous baby."

At Jessie's greeting, Theo was forced to cling to the counter like it was his sanity. "Hey."

Jessie cast a quick look around before his whiskey gaze landed on Theo again, weakening his knees. "May I talk to you alone?"

"You have to be fucking kidding me. You know Jessie Thunder?"

Theo and Jessie both ignored William's exclamation and question. Their eyes never wavered from staring at each other.

"Ezra told me never to let anyone talk to me alone here."

Jessie's forehead furrowed. "Even me?"

Theo fought the urge to laugh hysterically... or cry. "Probably especially you."

Jessie rolled his eyes. He motioned toward the end of the counter where they would be out of earshot. "At least move down here so I can give you your Christmas gift in private."

"You got me a gift?"

Jessie blinked as if taken aback by Theo's question. "Of course I did."

Theo couldn't say no after that. He headed to the opposite end of the counter. Jessie moved to join him. The bar between them was the only thing stopping Theo from hugging Jessie. He had never been happier to see anyone. "You look really good," Theo said the moment they had an ounce of privacy.

Jessie didn't respond to Theo's compliment. Instead, he handed Theo a brightly wrapped box. "Merry Christmas."

To Theo's horror, his hands shook slightly as he reached for the gift. He couldn't believe Jessie was really here and he had a present for Theo. He felt ridiculous. There was a ribbon tied around the box and Theo didn't want to break it. It was red and pretty. While Theo doubted Jessie had actually wrapped the gift himself, he still wanted to keep the bow. Thankfully, Jessie didn't call him on his sentimental actions. He finally managed to get the ribbon off the box without damaging it. From there, all he had to do was lift the lid. Theo stared down at the contents with his heart in his throat. It was a comic book. The brightly drawn image on the front was unmistakably Theo, ragged-looking and sitting sideways in the backseat of a police car.

"Thunder's Savior," Theo read aloud while lifting the comic from the box.

"It's our story," Jessie said, making Theo's throat swell. "I had it commissioned while I was in rehab."

Theo couldn't even speak as he flipped through

the pages. Scene after scene of them went by in a series of moments from their lives together. Theo stopped after a few pages. He already knew it didn't have a happy ending. He wanted to read it in private. Theo swallowed, trying to make his throat work. "This is the most amazing thing I've ever seen in my life." He finally managed to meet Jessie's stare. "Thank you. That doesn't sound adequate. I've missed you." Theo's voice cracked on the confession.

"I texted you countless times, but you never responded."

A humorless chuckle rose in Theo's throat at Jessie's claim. He had just wanted to yell at William for ignoring his texts. Now he was under the same spotlight. "I left the phone you gave me behind. It didn't seem right to act like I expected you to keep paying my phone bill after I moved in with Ezra."

Jessie looked a little more irritated by the second. "I told you I would take care of you."

That wasn't the point and Theo didn't know how to make Jessie understand. He couldn't let Jessie do anything for him, knowing their love didn't match. He knew Jessie loved him—maybe the way a person loved their best friend. Theo was ass over tea kettle in love with Jessie, and every day Jessie didn't love him back, Theo died a little more. If he stayed under

Jessie's roof and let Jessie keep supporting him while Jessie kept sleeping with everyone else, maybe one day Theo would hate him. That was the last thing Theo wanted.

There were so many things Theo wanted to say to that claim. The words clogged his brain and threatened to factory reset him. Theo chose to instead keep things light. "What were you doing with a phone in rehab anyhow? Don't they take everything, including your shoelaces?"

Jessie smiled. It was filled with laughter and Theo was lost. "I went to rich people rehab. It's not the same." Jessie's smile slipped away. "I have so much I want to say to you. Will you please let me?"

In the face of Jessie's open desperation, Theo found himself agreeing. "I'm off tomorrow. When I get up, I'll head over."

Jessie gave him a sharp nod. "That's all I can ask." He leaned his elbows on the counter, invading Theo's space. Theo automatically inhaled. He had missed the smell of Jessie's cologne. Missed Jessie. "Damn," Jessie breathed, sounding truly blown away. "You have no idea how much I've missed you."

It was like Theo was falling into Jessie's eyes. His body swayed toward Jessie, as if getting sucked closer to the other half of his soul.

Jessie took advantage. He shot forward and pressed his lips to Theo's. Theo sucked in a gasp. He had forgotten Jessie's taste. The weight of his lips. His feelings were so heavy they made it hard to breathe. Theo found himself tracing Jessie's jawline with the tip of his finger. He felt Jessie take a ragged breath against his lips. Nothing Jessie said to him could have been as powerful as that breath. Theo's eyes burned as he realized this was the first time Jessie had ever kissed him sober. Jessie wanting him had nothing to do with convenience. Theo wanted to curl up in a ball and cry, mourning everything he had lost.

"I'll see you in the morning."

Theo nodded, even though Jessie was already walking away. He watched him go with his heart in his throat. All the times Theo had told himself he wouldn't see Jessie again were out the window. Theo wondered if he would ever be free. It was possible he was simply too far gone. He had lost more than his heart when he met Jessie. Sometimes, Theo thought Jessie might have stolen his soul.

Cool air filled Jessie's lungs. He couldn't

recall the last time he took time to look at the stars. For the hundredth time, Jessie's hand lifted to his cheek. He could still feel Theo's finger tracing the line of his jaw. Slow. Sweet. Reverent. Tomorrow morning felt so far away. He wanted to text Theo, but Theo no longer had his phone. After learning that, he had gone straight home and to Theo's bedroom. Even the necklace Jessie had given him had been left behind. Theo hadn't taken a damn thing. Not the clothes nor the laptop. Even his shampoo was still in the shower. Jessie knew he could trust Ezra to take care of Theo. In fact, Theo looked amazing. It was obvious Ezra had been feeding him. He had filled out some and looked delicious, but Jessie wanted to be the reason Theo looked healthy. Goddamn, Jessie ached to be with him. He missed their talks. The sound of Theo's laughter. Jessie felt empty without him.

Jessie settled deeper into the lounge by the pool. He knew he should go inside and get some sleep. His counselor had stressed keeping a regular daily schedule. Jessie saw her point. His skin felt too tight. He already missed the oblivion. Inside, the walls had been closing in and choking the life from him. Jessie didn't know how to be sober and alone. He would figure it out, because he couldn't fail the people who loved him, but he also couldn't go inside.

"Do you have a single person on your security team who does anything but eat your food?"

An out-of-control smile tugged at Jessie's lips at the sound of Theo's voice. He turned his head. Theo stood, clutching the gift box Jessie had given him earlier and wearing the same clothes—like he hadn't bothered to go home before coming straight to Jessie. He had never been happier to see anyone in his life. "No one would stop you from coming onto the property. This is still your home. Your bedroom is still waiting. I've had Declan make sure your favorite foods are always stocked. Everything is just waiting for you to come back, including me."

Theo didn't move any closer. "If I hadn't left when I did, you might not have almost died. I could've stopped you."

Jessie's felt his forehead furrow. He didn't understand how Theo could think such a thing. "Oh, baby. You don't really believe that, do you?" Jessie sat up. He patted the lounge. "Come here."

Theo did as told, but he didn't loosen his hold on the box he hugged to his chest. Something about that twisted at Jessie's heart. He couldn't let Theo believe for one second that he had ever had any part in

Jessie's addictions. The problem was, he didn't really know how to make Theo understand no one could fix him except him. He just picked a place and started talking.

"Listen, gorgeous. Nothing I've done is on you." Jessie blew out a breath. Even to his ears, Jessie sounded like he was spouting pandering bullshit. "Did you ever Google me?"

Theo's beautiful blue eyes swung Jessie's way. "No. You asked me not to, so I didn't."

A smile snapped to Jessie's lips. Damn. He really loved Theo. "Maybe you should, after all. Can I ask you a favor?"

"Sure. Anything." Theo's immediate agreement was adorable.

"Will you come to bed with me? We don't have to do anything. I'm just having a really hard time tonight. They told me I should try to stick to a schedule, but the walls are closing in on me."

Theo stood and headed for the house. "Come on."

While trying to hide his ridiculous smile, Jessie followed closely on Theo's heels. Once inside the kitchen, Theo headed the wrong direction—like he planned to go to his old bedroom. Jessie paused.

"Where are you going? My room is this way," he said, motioning toward the opposite direction.

Theo turned his head from side to side, looking first down the hall and then back toward the living room where Jessie pointed. "Really? I always thought your room was right next to mine."

Jessie shook his head. "Declan's room is next to yours. I put you next to him so he could keep an eye on you for a few nights when you first moved in. That way, you couldn't sneak away from me. My bedroom is connected to my studio. That way, if inspiration strikes in the middle of the night, I can wander into my studio, fuck around, and not disturb anyone."

Theo's furrowed forehead didn't clear away. He shook his head and followed Jessie to the studio and then through another door to his bedroom. Theo paused just inside the doorway and looked around. "I never even noticed this door. Your bedroom is nothing like I expected."

Jessie glanced around at his small bedroom. It was pretty sparse. King-sized bed. Nightstand. Dresser. Bathroom. Closet. He didn't really need anything else. "What were you expecting besides it being on the opposite side of the house?"

Theo shrugged. "Now that I think about it, I

should've pictured this. You always take care of everyone else and keep nothing for yourself."

"I feel like I should be somewhat insulted."

Theo didn't smile like he'd hoped. In fact, he wouldn't even meet Jessie's gaze. "Can I ask you something that is completely none of my business?"

Jessie didn't need to think about it. "Everything is your business. Ask away."

Theo finally met his stare. He looked intense—like he needed to see Jessie answer, so he could judge for himself if Jessie lied. "When was the last time you had sex?"

Jessie blinked. He hadn't been expecting that one. Jessie stood by his earlier boast. Everything was Theo's business, but this one was a little touchy for him. It was humiliating to admit that he had been too messed up to get it up for longer than he could remember. "Hmm," Jessie hummed, struggling to remember. "I think I last tried about a year and a half ago." Jessie moved to pull the covers down on his bed and started stripping down to his underwear.

"Tried?"

Jessie took the gift box from Theo and set it on the dresser. "Yes. Tried. You've never been an addict. It's hard to get it up or keep it up when you've got so much chemical in your blood that there's no reason you're still moving at all." Jessie shrugged as he went to work, stealing Theo's shirt. "Most guys didn't care. They just wanted to tell people they took me home. But they care once you start puking in their bed. So, eventually, I stopped pretending I cared about anything other than losing myself in a high and stayed home." Jessie held Theo's stare. "And then, you came to me, and I started craving something else again. You are the first thing I've needed more than my trip." Jessie unbuttoned Theo's jeans. "Come to bed with me. Let me hold you. Help me sleep. Tomorrow, I will tell you anything you want to know."

"Okay." Theo sounded nervous.

Even though Jessie was literally throbbing with lust, he truly only wanted to hold Theo. He slid down Theo's zipper, trying not to brush the erection Theo could not hide. "Damn, you're beautiful," Jessie breathed. "Your gorgeous heart makes me want to be better."

Theo's gaze dropped to Jessie's lips before snapping back to Jessie's eyes. He visibly swallowed. "I know you need sleep, but would it be okay if I kissed you?"

Jessie could barely breathe through the thick desire. "Please?"

Theo didn't move fast. He took a step closer while staring at Jessie's mouth. By the time Theo's lips tentatively touched Jessie's, Jessie's patience was gone. He shoved both hands inside the back of Theo's jeans, diving inside his underwear. Jessie squeezed Theo's ass, kneading as he hauled Theo against him. He kissed and bit as he tugged at Theo's clothes. It wasn't until Theo was nude, had his legs wrapped around Jessie's waist, and Jessie was headed toward the bed that Jessie calmed a hair. His kiss lightened as he set one knee on the bed and lowered Theo to the mattress. Even as aroused as Jessie was, he held on to a modicum of sense. He wouldn't move too fast. This wasn't about sex. The unnatural amount of love and desire that Jessie felt toward Theo needed to be cherished. He needed to be closer to him.

Theo pushed Jessie's underwear down his hips. "I'm not asking for anything," he whispered. "Just your skin against mine."

There was so much bravery in that small request, considering how badly Jessie had hurt him. Jessie wouldn't let him down. He shifted positions and peeled off his underwear before covering Theo's body with his. Theo sucked in a breath as Jessie straddled him and their erections met. Jessie kissed the tip of Theo's nose. Theo stared up at him with so much love and trust that Jessie's eyes stung. Jessie rocked, incapable of staying still. A loud gasp escaped Theo. Jessie did it again. The friction between their bodies felt so good. Jessie linked fingers with Theo, stared down into his eyes, and thrust. The pressure against his cock wasn't anywhere near enough, yet it was maddeningly perfect. Jessie's hips rolled, seeking more pleasure. Theo gasped and whimpered beneath him, accepting the frustrating way Jessie made love to him.

"You look so turned on," Jessie whispered without thought. He couldn't stop. "Just beautiful and aggravated." A smile pulled at Jessie's lips. "I don't want to look away. I want to watch you come." Theo tried biting back a moan. It came out smothered-sounding. Jessie couldn't have that. He changed angles and ground down, dragging a cry from Theo. "Fuck, yeah," Jessie growled, wanting more. "Don't hide, Theo. Give me your pleasure. I want to hear it."

Theo whimpered.

Something inside Jessie snapped. He needed to taste that sound. His mouth slammed down on Theo's as he reached between and pumped. He held their cocks together and thrust, losing all patience. Theo cried out around their entwined tongues. Hot cum gushed between them, soaking Jessie's skin. Jessie focused on the way Theo shook and the building pressure. He pictured himself buried in Theo's virgin ass. A loud gasp burst from him as ecstasy punched him. His body shook as cum shot from his dick, pouring onto Theo. The knowledge that it was Theo beneath him had Jessie's mind a complete mess. He fought, saying all the words that crowded his brain. Theo hadn't agreed to come home. He hadn't said they were a couple. Theo had simply agreed to stay with him tonight. Jessie's sanity was too fragile. He couldn't let himself slip or hope. Jessie had a lot of making up to do. He couldn't expect Theo to pretend Jessie hadn't been a complete piece of shit since the day they met.

As their tongues stroked and their hands fought to feel every inch of each other, an unusual sensation filled Jessie. It had been so long since he felt this way that it took him a minute to decipher the emotion. It was hope. Jessie hadn't possessed an ounce of hope in so goddamn long, he wanted to cry. Theo had done that. He was the one who saved Jessie in more ways than one. Jessie would fight to keep him right here where he belonged—under Jessie's roof and beneath his body. First, he would let the boy sleep. Then, tomorrow, Jessie would give him the world.

WHILE DRAGGING HIS FINGERTIPS UP AND DOWN the back of Jessie's arm that was draped over Theo's body, Theo stared at the ceiling wide awake. Jessie's deep breathing sounded peaceful. Theo felt full. Of all the times he imagined making love to Jessie, Theo never pictured that. He had expected more. Theo had certainly expected a lot more pain on his part. He hadn't pictured their bodies moving together the way they had—beautiful, like making music. Still, Theo kind of wanted the pain. He didn't think he would feel like he had gotten as close as he possible could to Jessie until Jessie was buried inside him.

Theo turned his head and stared at Jessie's sleeping face. He looked relaxed. Younger. Theo smiled. He was sickeningly in love with this man. Theo wanted to know every detail of his life. He fought the urge to wake Jessie and beg for his every story. Theo's gaze slid toward the dresser at the thought of stories. He had been so hellbent on getting to Jessie after work, Theo hadn't taken the time to read the comic Jessie had made for him. An overwhelming need to know slammed into Theo. There was no way in hell he would sleep anytime soon.

While moving slow and trying not to wake Jessie, Theo slipped from beneath Jessie's arm and out of bed. For a moment, he stood completely still, making sure Jessie didn't wake before rushing to grab his underwear and the box. He carried both into the studio. After pulling on his underwear, Theo sat on the floor and took the lid off the box. His breath came out sounding shaky as he turned the first page on the comic. Theo's eyes burned from not wanting to blink. He eyed every line and detail of each picture. They were so true to life, Jessie had to have given the artist pictures of Theo to be this accurate. He smiled at the way they captured how Theo and Jessie always seemed to sway toward one another when talking and how they always sat too close. His smile grew at a picture of their fingers accidentally brushing followed by an image of them looking at each other in surprise. As he got deeper into the story, things grew darker. Storm clouds brewed over Jessie's head and hints of a past tragedy haunted him. His thoughts grew uglier as he realized he had dragged Theo down into a pit with him. Tears gathered in Theo's eyes as he read about Jessie purposely overdosing and Theo bringing him back to life. A hot tear landed on Theo's leg as he went through rehab with Jessie in the story and read the text messages Theo wouldn't answer. By the time he reached the final page, tears flowed freely down his cheeks. The last page was a single image. Jessie's phone with one final unread message to Theo.

Theo jumped to his feet. He had to know. Theo forgot about his lack of clothing. Nothing mattered but seeing that message for himself. Luckily, he didn't run across anyone as he headed to his old bedroom. Everything was where he had left it. His phone sat on top of his closed laptop on the nightstand. Theo grabbed it and plugged it in, waiting for it to charge enough to start. After what felt like forever but was probably only seconds, ding after ding sounded as incoming messages made themselves known. Theo held his breath. There it was. The final message from Jessie.

Jessie: *I love you.*

Theo sniffed so hard, it hurt his throat. If anyone had ever said those words to him, Theo had been too young to recall. He fought the urge to rush back to Jessie's room and force him to say them to Theo's face. Instead, he picked up the necklace Jessie had given him and put it back on. This was his home. He replied to Jessie's message and then opened his web browser. Theo typed Jessie's name. He didn't have to hunt. It was the first headline he saw.

Jessie Thunder enters rehab two years after the death...

Theo clicked when the headline stopped there. He read from the top.

Jessie Thunder, the superstar drummer who made millions after shooting to the top of billboards around the world, entered rehab Sunday morning. Almost two years to the day after three of Thunder's band mates were found dead after ingesting drugs laced with fentanyl, Jessie has been admitted to...

Theo read with this heart in his throat. Bits and pieces from the story leapt out.

Thunder was the only survivor of the unfortunate overdose...

Thunder recounted the story of waking up among the bodies of his best friends and band mates...

Theo's eyes fell closed for a moment before he tried to read deeper, getting back to the present story.

... *He was found unresponsive and revived by an unnamed friend of the family.*

Theo couldn't take anymore. He shut down his phone and headed back down the hall. Thankfully, Jessie hadn't budged. Theo spent a moment staring at his sleeping form. Ezra had said Theo could stay with him for the rest of his life if he wanted. It was as an offer Theo would have to decline. His place was here. Jessie needed him. Jessie needed Theo's love and watchful eye. Theo wouldn't let him hurt or be alone. He especially wouldn't let Jessie backslide. It was time to heal. Jessie was his. Theo had him. He would be Jessie's strength.

Theo stripped and slipped back into bed. Jessie stirred and rolled onto his back. He snagged Theo and brought him with him. With Jessie settled on his back with Theo in his arms, Theo pressed his ear to Jessie's chest. The steady beat of Jessie's heart soothed him. Jessie loved him. He loved Theo so much, he had chosen to get clean, even though being clean meant facing a nightmarish past. That was some heady knowledge. It was a big responsibility. Theo wanted it. From this night on, Jessie would only know happiness. He would see. Theo wouldn't fail him.

TEN

For a long while, Jessie watched Theo sleep. He looked so sexy with his shaggy hair in his eyes and face sleep swollen. Jessie was wide awake and painfully turned on. Theo was an irresistible sight to wake up to. Jessie's lower back screamed at him to move. Lounging around all day no longer suited his body. Jessie rolled and checked the time on his phone. There was one unread message waiting. A smile stretched his lips when he saw it was from Theo. He quickly tapped the message icon.

Theo: *I love you too.*

That was it. Jessie couldn't wait any longer. He slowly slid the drawer open on his bedside table, hoping Theo wouldn't wake. Every move he made sounded loud as hell in the otherwise silent room. He found the lube and coated his fingers. Jessie wouldn't go all in today, but Theo needed a little practice. Plus, Jessie wanted to show him how much pleasure his body could manage.

Jessie kissed Theo's back as his lubed fingers found Theo's asshole. He probed, going deep and right for the spot that would drive him wild. A loud moan vibrated from Theo. He arched into Jessie's touch, seeking more. Jessie kissed his way down Theo's spine before urging him to roll over. He wanted Theo's dick. The second Theo was on his back, Jessie settled between his thighs and went back to fucking Theo with his fingers. He mimicked sex, pumping his wet digits in and out of Theo as he swallowed Theo's cock. Theo's hips left the bed.

"Oh, god. Don't stop," Theo whispered, sending Jessie's lust skyrocketing.

Jessie fought the urge to hump the bed like a teenage boy. He was so horny, and Theo was so fucking tight and responsive. Theo was like a man's wet dream come true. Jessie wanted to shove his dick inside Theo and pound until they were both too raw to walk. Months and months, he had craved. Even when Jessie's body wouldn't work, his brain had been just fine. He had never had any trouble imagining this boy on his cock, sucking and riding. Goddamn, he was turned on past the point of insanity.

Jessie sucked Theo's dick like he would be the one who came. He couldn't stop. Theo was tugging his hair and incoherently babbling. Theo's body tensed. Jessie sucked harder. Cum filled his mouth as a cry reverberated from his bedroom walls. Jessie squeezed his eyes closed and swallowed as much as he could. His cock ached, but his heart was full. Nothing mattered to him except pleasing Theo.

Theo tugged his hair, urging him higher. Jessie kissed his way up Theo's body. Before he reached Theo's mouth, he caught sight of the necklace Theo wore. His heart twisted in his chest. Jessie pressed a light kiss to the musical note resting on Theo's collarbone. His eyes burned. Jessie found himself burying his face in the crook of Theo's neck and fighting tears.

"I love you. Jesus, Theo. I knew I had lost you and I wanted to die." Jessie swallowed hard as a panic attack threatened to pull him under. "You're the only thing keeping me sane. I can't lose you."

"Shhh." Theo rubbed his back and massaged his head while tears slipped from Jessie without his permission. "I love you, sweetie. I'm not going anywhere."

Jessie's body slowly relaxed beneath Theo's soothing touch. His lips skimmed Theo's throat for the hundredth time. "Thank you." Jessie tried to move, but he started shaking unexpectedly.

Theo's hold tightened on him. "I've got you. Just let me carry it for a minute."

Jessie relaxed again, giving up the fight. It felt too good in Theo's arms for a panic attack to win. Sometimes, they came from nowhere. He didn't do well with stress anymore. Not since waking up alone and surrounded by lifeless eyes. Jessie drew a steady breath. He could feel Theo's heart beating against him. Theo wasn't like the out-of-control people who had always surrounded him. He was steady. Strong. His spirit was unbreakable. In Theo's arms, Jessie recognized he would be okay. They just needed time and each other. Everything else would find a way. Jessie believed that with all his heart. He had to.

As hard as Theo tried, and despite Jessie's momentary panic attack, he couldn't stop smiling. Life had been shit for much longer than most people were forced to endure. Now everything felt different. He felt like everything would—finally—be okay.

Theo's eyes fell closed as Jessie's lips brushed his neck.

"Run away with me."

Theo chuckled at the suggestion.

Jessie leaned back and met his stare. He looked adorably intense. "I'm being serious. Let's go to Aspen and lock ourselves in a cabin. We can light a fire in the fireplace and focus on each other. I've missed the fuck out of you. I don't want to share you with anyone or anything else right now."

Theo wanted the picture Jessie painted, but he also needed to be realistic. "What about Ezra and my job? Ezra just got you back too and Wrecker needs my help. Plus, Declan and Johnny have missed you too. I'm sure they're looking forward to spending some time with you."

Jessie didn't back down. "Ezra will understand. He's my brother and we love each other, but he also gets that you're the biggest part of me now. As to working, do you really plan to keep working?"

A hint of irritation wormed its way into Theo's ridiculous happiness. "Maybe I do. I don't know. I mean, maybe. Ugh. I can't leave Wrecker high and dry no matter what we decide. He gave me a job when I didn't feel like I had anything else."

Jessie stared at him with a crushing mixture of

understanding and disappointment. "Okay." He immediately brightened again. "What if I send someone to cover for you until you decide if you're going back? That way, Wrecker will have the help he needs, and you'll have some time to decide if I'm worth giving another chance."

"Oh, sweetie." Theo cupped Jessie's cheeks. "I've already decided you're never getting away from me." A smile tugged at Theo's lips. "I think you forget that you saved me first. That's what we do. We rescue each other. What about Declan and Johnny?"

Jessie looked excited—like he knew he would soon have his way. "I think we'll probably need Johnny, since I still have reporters stalking me everywhere I go, but I'll put him in a cabin nearby or something so we can still be alone. As to Declan, he always takes six weeks off at Christmas to travel around the country. I saw him for a little while when he picked me up from rehab before he headed out. We're used to touring and he misses it. We'll see each other when he gets back." A pained look crossed Jessie's face. "If he even wants to keep working for me. He seemed kind of sick of my shit when we talked yesterday. It's okay, though. He lasted longer than I expected. Hurting people and driving them away is what I do." Jessie's gaze locked on to Theo again with the same intensity he had while asking Theo to run away. "That bullshit is over, though. I swear I'll never hurt you again. I'm in this. All the way."

Theo was torn between telling Jessie the truth about Declan to save him from thinking any of Declan's bullshit was on Jessie, and keeping Ezra's secrets. He chose option three. Distraction. "If you're in this for good, do you ever plan to make love to me?"

Jessie's expression underwent a hilarious series of transformations before landing on confused. "I made love to you last night and I don't know anyone who complains about waking up to a blow job."

Theo felt the blush on his cheeks, but he didn't back down. He stroked Jessie's erection that had been poking him all morning like it tried to get Theo's attention. "I'm not complaining. I'm telling you that I want this inside me, and I want to know if you plan for that to happen anytime soon."

A flush rose high on Jessie's cheeks. His eyes looked unfocused as Theo continued stroking his cock. "I've been trying to ease you into things," Jessie said after a moment—like his attention was split. Theo squeezed. He needed Jessie's pleasure. "Oh, god."

"I'm not afraid." Nervous, yes. Theo wasn't completely out of his depth. He had done some solo play. It was a little different with someone looking at him and making him worry he would do something stupid or humiliating.

"I won't make it to being inside you if you keep doing that," Jessie said, sounding breathless

when Theo squeezed again.

For a moment, Theo was torn. He kind of wanted to make Jessie blow before he was ready, but Theo really didn't want to miss his chance to feel Jessie pushing inside him. In the end, he released Jessie. "Hurry. Find a condom."

Jessie scrambled away like he didn't need to be told twice. A chuckle stuck in Theo's throat. It died as he watched Jessie suit up. His mouth watered as Jessie rolled the condom down his length and coated it with lube. His body practically vibrated with desire—like Jessie hadn't sucked him dry earlier.

While squirting more lube on his fingers, Jessie eyed Theo. "I don't want to hurt you."

"You won't."

Jessie crawled between Theo's thighs. "Just let me play for a little while to make sure."

Theo's head fell back against the pillow. A moan rose in his throat as Jessie's lubed fingers found their way inside his ass again. He was back to stretching and hitting that button that drove him wild. Theo fought the urge to stroke his own cock and lost. A pained sound vibrated from Jessie as Theo jacked off —like Theo was killing him. A second finger joined the first. Theo's hips left the bed. He didn't know if he would make it until Jessie could get inside him. A third finger stretched him. Theo whimpered. He needed more.

"Please, Jessie."

"Goddamn. You're perfect." That was all the warning Theo got before he found himself impaled.

It hurt, but nowhere near as much as he expected. He recognized Jessie hadn't given him time to tense and that had probably saved him. Then Jessie rocked, hitting the perfect spot with his dick, and Theo couldn't be still. He fought to get closer to Jessie. They were one person. Completely connected. Theo was a mess. His body was a huge combination of pain and ecstasy while his soul recognized he was complete. His other half was a part of him. Theo was in love and on the verge of orgasm. The mixture was a heady one. Theo would do anything Jessie asked in that moment if he promised to make Theo always feel like this.

"I love you." The confession tore from Theo's

lips as he reached for orgasm. Everything felt too good, especially his heart.

"Then marry me."

Theo went from being a half second away from orgasm to frozen. He stared at Jessie. Jessie was still buried inside him and he looked completely calm—like this wasn't a whim.

Jessie massaged every place he could reach while he waited for Theo's answer. When Theo couldn't find his voice, Jessie pushed. "I'm serious, Theo. Marry me. Let Aspen be our honeymoon. I love you and I think I have since the moment I set eyes on you. You're the one for me."

"Okay." It definitely wasn't the marriage proposal of his dreams, if he had ever thought to dream of such a thing, but it was still magical. The way Jessie lit at his response, and then fell on Theo like a man possessed, made all the romantic gestures in the world look dull. Jessie kissed Theo deep as he rocked inside him, hitting the right spot while creating all the friction between them. Theo's entire body burned. He focused on the pleasure, letting it grow. Then, the spring that had been winding tight broke. Theo's body jerked. An orgasm rocked him, tearing a cry from his throat. Jessie threw his head back and strained. Theo couldn't look away as Jessie came. It was beautiful. His eyes stung. They were beautiful. Maybe they had started out in the oddest of ways and found love where no one else would have, but they were right together. Theo wouldn't let doubt destroy them again. They would show the world how much true love could survive.

ELEVEN

Jessie loved Aspen. He couldn't recall the last time he had seen snow. Not that Theo and he had seen much of anything other than the inside of their cabin. They were truly newlyweds in every way. Jessie freely admitted he couldn't keep his hands to himself and had no plans on trying. He did feel a bit guilty about one thing, though. They hadn't told anyone other than Ezra they were getting married. In fact, they had well and truly eloped. They had packed their bags, snagged Johnny, and shown up on Ezra's doorstep. They had married in Ezra's living room before sneaking away to Colorado.

Jessie promised Ezra they would have a big wedding later and let Ezra plan the entire event. Hopefully, that would appease everyone who would be hurt by their need for privacy. Jessie just didn't have a big wedding in him right now. While he was better, some days were still hard. Stress still wasn't his friend. Thankfully, Theo turned his body to jelly and kept him totally relaxed... except when he had Jessie hard, which Jessie was in danger of right now while watching Theo pour their hot chocolate. That was it. That was all it took, and Jessie was a mess.

Theo smiled as he carried two cups Jessie's way. His hair was a mess and he wore only flannel pajama pants. He was the most beautiful thing Jessie had ever set eyes upon in all his years of living. Theo handed Jessie one of the cups before joining him on the floor in front of the fireplace. "Where were we?"

A smile tugged at the corners of Jessie's mouth. "You were at the part where the bad guy was about to give his monologue."

With a nod, Theo picked up the comic book. He gave Jessie a very schoolteacher-like look over the edge of the book. "Remember our deal. Three more pages and then you have to write. Extended honeymoon or not, I'm not letting you give up your dreams. Okay?"

Jessie bit his bottom lip to stop himself from smiling like an idiot. "Okay."

With a sharp nod, Theo went back to reading

while Jessie stared at his mouth and didn't hear a word. Theo didn't realize it, but he was the only one who hadn't stopped believing in him. No one else thought Jessie had any songs left in him to write. Everyone else on the planet believed Jessie's musical talent had died with his band. While it was true he wouldn't likely play on stage ever again, Theo hadn't stopped pushing him to create. That was real love. It was a love only another artist understood. Jessie didn't think Theo realized it, but he had a creative genius living inside him too.

"You should start narrating comic books online. I love listening to you. I can't think I'm the only one who would love to listen to you all the time. You're a natural at voice acting."

Theo blushed and kept reading. Jessie knew Theo meant to pretend Jessie had never suggested such a thing. Unfortunately for Theo, the idea was already in Jessie's head. He would push Theo toward something he loved, because Theo would do the same for him. Jessie couldn't stop staring at him. Love damn near choked Jessie. When Theo had holed up in Jessie's pool house, Jessie never dreamed that dirty and homeless kid would burrow his way inside Jessie's heart and set up shop. It just went to show that no one knew who would be set in their path to save them. He couldn't imagine his life without Theo now. But Jessie knew one thing with absolute certainty, he would never have to live without him again. They were written in the stars.

Keep an eye out for the next Candied Crush, *Beautifully Angelic.*

Please consider leaving a review on Amazon. Reviews really help with a book's visibility, which ensures I can continue writing. Thank you, Charity.

ABOUT THE AUTHOR

Charity Parkerson is an award winning and multi-published author with several companies. Born with no filter from her brain to her mouth, she decided to take this odd quirk and insert it in her characters.

*Eight-time Readers' Favorite Award Winner

*2015 Passionate Plume Award Finalist

*2013 Reviewers' Choice Award Winner

*2012 ARRA Finalist for Favorite Paranormal Romance

*Five-time winner of The Mistress of the Darkpath

Connect with her online:

—Sign up for my newsletter: http://bit.ly/CharityNews

—Join my readers' group on Facebook: http://bit.ly/CharitysTribe

—Website: charityparkerson.com

—Facebook:
facebook.com/authorCharityParkerson

facebook.com/TheMenofSin

—Twitter: twitter.com/CharityParkerso

—Instagram: Instagram.com/sinnerauthor

www.ingramcontent.com/pod-product-compliance
Lightning Source LLC
LaVergne TN
LVHW020046110826
845155LV00029B/649

* 9 7 8 1 9 4 6 0 9 9 7 1 6 *